HOUSE OF DECAY

EMMA D. THOMPSON

HOUSE OF DECAY

A novel by Emma D. Thompson

Cover designed by Alexander Stott

Author photo taken by Sarah Feldhut

For my mom and dad,

who always believed I could

ONE

Beyond the sleepy town of Halsbrook, where the foliage was so dense it stopped carriages in their tracks, and the path was both winding and treacherous, there loomed a great manor house where the forest met the sea. Standing at three stories tall, it dwarfed the large oak trees littering the property. The dozens of windows that spotted the house's façade were empty eye sockets in the night, gaping and ever watchful.

Acres of wild woods, stuffed with dark rivers and thick underbrush, blanketed most of the estate. The family cemetery, just beyond the tree line, was a maze of cracking headstones and wilting statues. A rickety, wrought iron fence kept the wilderness at bay, but just barely. The burial ground was mostly unkempt except for the grave of William Halsby, builder of the house. A large granite angel with arms outstretched stood watch over his plot, somehow untouched by the elements and the wearing of time.

The Halsby family had been the house's guardian and caretaker for almost a century. The façade looked both decaying and unchanged since its building in 1750. The plants grew with such fervor it was difficult not to become tangled in them as one walked the grounds. Items left outside could be quickly swallowed by twisting vines. Even the poor servant boy had been wrapped in its spindly branches, trapped and then forgotten, only to be found in the following weeks when he had started to smell.

There was a distinctive change in weather upon entering the front gate, colder and wetter, like an invisible cloud hung over the property and all that was near it. The house itself was massive. Dozens of chimneys and large spires decorated the roof with no semblance of order. Brown stones made up the sidings, but most of it was covered in a thick layer of moss or ivy, giving the house a green glow.

Viviann Clarke hated the manor the moment she laid eyes on it. She emerged from the carriage almost as green as the house. The small bit of breakfast she had managed to get down that morning threatened to resurface. She pulled her cloak closer against the bitter air, feeling the eyes of the house on her like pinpricks. Peter, her new husband, extended his arm.

"Welcome home," he said. She noticed sweat pooling on his brow, despite the cool weather. Was he that nervous?

His sincerity fell over her like a warm blanket. As she hovered between the carriage and her new husband, she looked from him to the house, whose imposing shadow shrouded them in near darkness. She took Peter's arm.

On the front lawn stood the staff, frozen to the bone, dressed in stark white linen and drooping faces. There was more of them than she could count, but four stood to the forefront. All but one were much older than the rest of the staff, and their shoulders sagged under the cloudy sky.

"This, my dear, is the estate's butler, Benson," Peter said, standing back so Viviann could introduce herself.

Unsure of what to do and caught off guard by the word "dear," Viviann gave a quick nod to the overweight gentleman. She recognized him from the ceremony. Peter led her to the woman standing next to Benson; she had greying hair and deep lines scrawled into her tan skin. She looked as unremarkable as an older Englishwoman could be.

"This is the head housekeeper, Mrs. Avery," Peter said without even stopping, carrying on to the next.

Viviann tried to nod to each of them so she wouldn't appear rude, but they didn't even seem to notice her. They stared ahead with empty eyes. It seemed like they were standing for a funeral, not a welcoming party to their Lord's new wife.

Peter sped through the greetings with Viviann's lady's maid and the Head Groundskeeper before pulling her towards the front door, where a footman was already standing, awaiting their entrance. The servant's tails alone were probably more expensive and better kept than the dress she was wearing.

"Lady Halsby's things are in the carriage and will need to be unpacked," Peter said to no one in particular, distant and curt. "If you have trouble finding her a dress before dinner, please lay out one of Lady Elizabeth's."

Elizabeth? Who was that? Viviann wondered. She looked down at herself, slightly wrinkled after the carriage ride. It was the nicest dress she owned. Perhaps this Elizabeth character, whoever that was, had something more suitable for this house.

Peter turned to Viviann. The servants looked at her as well.

"Yes, thank you very much," Viviann offered. Peter simply walked on.

The staff were already shuffling away towards the servant's entrance when Viviann turned back to them, and for a moment she stood there alone.

"Quickly, dear, there is so much to see."

There was that "dear" again. Viviann turned towards her new home and crossed the threshold into the dark interior.

TWO

The house was magnificent, although obviously old. The front door gave way to an immense foyer, where a crystal chandelier hung from the tall ceiling. Marble tile covered the long stretch of space, although it looked dinghy in the half light. Thick curtains hid the monstrous windows by the front door, so the entryway seemed dark and mysterious. Ornately carved arched doorways flanked the room on both sides, leading to the other great rooms of the house.

"The house lacks a formal ballroom, so we've always just held them here," Peter explained. His voice echoed in the near empty space, as did the clicks of their shoes.

The great staircase was indeed great, made up of dozens of red carpeted steps, with a thick cherry wood banister that was carved with peculiar cherubs and angels. Viviann ran her hands along it when they ventured up the stairs, feeling the crevices of each pair of eyes and mouths.

Thick padded carpet and patterned wallpaper covered every floor and wall in the rest of the house, save for the hardwood-lined hallways, which looked bizarre compared with every other room. Catching a glimpse of the long corridors, Viviann could imagine herself becoming completely turned around, as they looked identical. Instead of detailed wallpaper, the walls in these places were stuffed with paintings. She recognized one to be Peter as a younger man, when he must've been eighteen or so. He looked broader in the portrait, as regal as a prince, but his face was solemn and rounded like that of a sad child. He resembled Edward here, and her heart crumpled at the thought. Edward was the man she had intended to marry, before he fell ill and was taken from her. She remembered a similar painting hanging in Edward's house, next to the stairs. He told her they would have an equally embarrassing portrait of their son hanging in their own house someday. Viviann walked on as the lump in her throat grew larger.

Eventually they found their way to Peter's study, which was dark and messy, but it was the only room that felt lived in or loved. The mess on his desk and the forgotten teacups pilled along the bookshelves made the room intimate, like she was peeking into Peter's soul. He seemed the most relaxed in this room. Before doing anything else, he showed her a picture frame that hung in the corner. It was a letter with worn edges and small tears, written in sloppy writing.

"This here," Peter said, tapping the glass, "was from my grandfather to my father, when it was time for him to inherit the house. My father passed it on to me and I'll pass..."

Peter trailed off but Viviann filled in the blanks. The sentimentality of their wedding was wearing off quick. She had a role to play.

Viviann leaned in close to the letter before they left. It looked like nothing but the ravings of a madman to her.

"This house is the legacy of the Halsby family," Peter recited with a proud smile as he held the door open.

After her master tour, and when her feet were aching, Viviann found herself alone in her dressing room with a promise that her lady's maid would be at her service any moment. Viviann looked around. The two trunks she brought were already here, and her clothes were arranged in piles. The high ceilings, the deep blue wallpaper, the velvet wingback chairs that stood before the floor to ceiling windows, it was all too much. It was not at all what Viviann was used to, and she cringed at her reflection when she caught it in the ornate mirror above her new white dresser. In a room like this she looked positively peasant-like. Even in a gown as expensive as the one she was wearing. What was she doing here? Why did she ever agree to this?

Viviann jumped when her lady's maid entered the room, carrying an array of silk under her arm. She looked as surprised as Viviann felt, like she had forgotten she was here. The woman standing in front of her couldn't have been but a few years older than herself. She had her raven hair pulled back into a tight bun, and her dark brows furrowed.

"Come this way, my lady." The maid walked to the double armoire and opened the doors, where at least fifty different dresses were organized on cloth-wrapped hangers.

When Viviann came closer, she saw the armoire was crammed, filled with things like fine jewelry, hair pieces, as well as hats, bonnets, and day gloves, like a lady was already living here. Viviann didn't recognize any of the items as her own.

"There must be another trunk downstairs since I never found your dinner dresses," the maid said. She laid out the silk pieces she had been holding, revealing them to be various colors of long dinner gloves, glossy in the candlelight.

Viviann internally sighed, knowing there were no more trunks of hers to be found. Instead of admitting this, she nodded and allowed the maid to undress her like any true lady would, standing straight-backed and staring ahead. The maid started with the clasps on the back of her dress. She worked in silence for many minutes, swift and efficient, pulling out a gown and replacing the one Viviann was wearing faster than Viviann could've done on her own. The gown itself indeed looked like something suitable for a dinner here, with the many ruffles and elaborate beading along the bodice, but the color reminded her of vomit. The maid didn't ask her what she thought, however, so Viviann stayed quiet.

"You must think me quite rude," Viviann said, offering her hand to be slipped into a cream-colored glove. "I didn't have a chance to ask you your name earlier."

"Mrs. Winslet. But everyone here calls me Evelyn. You're all set, my lady," Evelyn said without looking at her, already moving away to shut the armoire.

"Does your husband work here as well?" Viviann said to the maid's back.

"Oh...no, my lady. It is customary for lady's maids to be called 'Mrs.'"

Viviann stood there a moment more, feeling heat rise to her cheeks. Evelyn closed the doors of the armoire to reveal a reflection in the dark windows; Viviann noticed her face looked strained, like she was trying not to cry.

After a lavish six course dinner, filled with whitefish, clams, mussels, and a flaming cake that contained a strange and sweet jam inside, Viviann and Peter retired to the great room. Above the wide stone fireplace hung an immense painting of William Halsby. With a fire in the hearth, shadows flickered across the painting's face. Viviann sat on the edge of her seat, never turning away from the piece of art. There was something about it she couldn't look away from. The subject seemed like a hard man, rigid and stiff in his suit, sitting at the desk that now lay inside Peter's study, and what must have been William's study almost a century ago. The painter included all the clutter on William's desk, like piles of paper and books, and a teacup without a saucer close by. Just like Peter. In front of William was what looked like a leather-bound journal, wrapped in an extra string of uncured leather. What an odd thing to add to such a formal painting, Viviann thought.

Peter sat by her with a book in hand, as comfortable as could be -like he hadn't just married a stranger-, and completely oblivious to the hooded eyes of his ancestor. Viviann held her teacup with both hands, trying to siphon the small amount of heat that radiated from the piece of china, warming her icy fingers. She nudged closer to the fire until she was practically climbing over the sofa's arm. Her dress was tighter at the waist than she was used to, and when she moved, she felt the seams pull along the bodice.

She rested her cup on the ornate table in front of her and cleared her throat, a startling sound in the silent house.

"Peter, may I ask you something?" She waited until he put down his book to continue. She wanted to save her questions for the following morning but couldn't stop herself. The silence they sat through at dinner had made her anxious, and she wanted nothing more than to unload every thought that had popped into her head since she arrived.

"Who is Elizabeth?"

Peter contemplated this longer than she would have liked.

"She was my late wife," he finally said, his eyes drifting into memories. "We weren't married long."

"And when was that?" Viviann asked, trying to hide her shock. Her parents never said anything about him being a widower. A sharp pain stabbed at her chest, a deep familiar pain.

"Almost two years ago, actually. We were only married for a few months, though."

"What happened?" The painting's eyes now hovered behind her as she listened to her husband, and the feeling on the back of her neck was making her squirm.

"She died. Well, she killed herself. Horribly, in fact." He was utterly lost in thought now. Although he was right next to her, and his even voice was filling up the dim room, she felt as alone as one could be. Peter's eyes were so distant that she doubted he would notice if she stood up and walked away.

"How?" She whispered without reason. Why would anyone want to discuss something so horrible? Her mother would be fuming if she knew Viviann was continuing such a conversation.

"She cut her wrists in the bathtub."

The silence was deafening. Viviann stared down at her own wrists, protected by a layer of expensive silk and the silver bracelet her parents gave her on her eighteenth birthday, only two years ago. The same year Peter had married and lost his wife. The same year she met Edward. What a horrible way to go, Viviann thought.

"She was deeply unhappy here. I think she wasn't used to such a large house, and so few people to fill it."

Viviann looked up, as if she could see through the ceiling and into the floors above. She didn't doubt it could be lonely here. How many rooms were in this house? Twenty-five? More? She thought of their dinner at that impossibly large table that could seat twenty. She felt lonely already and she had only been here for a handful of hours.

"It was difficult at first, but it's easier now. I almost forget sometimes, I'm ashamed to say. You see, we didn't really know each other," Peter said with a nervous chuckle. She was amazed with his honesty, with his courage to articulate a pain that could hardly be described, only felt.

He looked sad, Viviann noticed. Not like he had lost someone dear to him, but like it was his fault.

"It was incredibly hard for the staff, especially her maid. She was the one that found Elizabeth."

Viviann couldn't help but picture it. She thought of the poor girl she met earlier; how small and frail she seemed. What a nightmare. When Edward passed, she awoke to find the bed drenched in sweat; she couldn't imagine what it would've been like if it was blood instead.

"Can I confess something?" Viviann asked after a long stretch of silence. She willed her voice to stay even, but it still came out shaky. Peter looked at her with his sad blue eyes.

"I was engaged before this." Viviann said. Unlike what her mother had thought, the world did not explode upon her whispering this truth. Peter knitted his eyebrows together.

"Before we could marry, he fell ill. Fever. He fought it for a long time, and we all thought he was going to push through." Viviann closed her eyes against the memories. "He didn't."

Peter was silent still, but he reached for her hand across the small stretch of space between their seats. They sat there together under the silent house until Benson came to check on them, a sure sign it was time to retreat to bed.

Later that night, while Peter lay on top of her, she couldn't help but wonder if he was thinking about Elizabeth. As hard as she tried, she couldn't stop herself from thinking about Edward. Peter hadn't looked at her since they started, instead pressing his face into the pillow next to hers. It was painful at first, performing her womanly duty, almost making her cry out, but it was better after a few minutes, and Viviann could almost close her eyes and pretend she liked it. She remembered sitting at the nondescript vanity in her family's room at the inn, just this morning. Viviann's mother had pinned her hair back in silence while her father and the carriage waited outside.

"Isn't there anything you need to tell me, mother?" Viviann had said. "About what to expect tonight?"

"Oh, for God's sake, Viviann, why do you have to make everything so dramatic? You lay there. It'll be over quickly. It's really not that hard."

Her mother was right, it was over quickly, and by the time he rolled over and blew out his bedside candle, she had just finished pulling down her nightgown.

As she lay in the darkness, Viviann felt the weight of a thousand bricks on her chest. Is this what it would be like if she had married Edward? She imagined feeling like her whole world would have been righted, like all the pieces of her heart would slide into place, complete. She felt hollow in the silence. This was her life now, she reminded herself.

A low growl sounded from upstairs, making her jump. At first, she wondered if it was the floor creaking under someone's feet, but the more she heard it, the more she was convinced it was the guttural voicings of a caged animal. Had an animal found its way into the house? As quick as it started, it stopped.

Peter was already asleep, again oblivious to the strangeness of his ancestral home. She must've been more tired than she first thought; tired enough to start hearing things. As Viviann tried giving into her exhaustion and heartache, she felt a knot form in the pit of her stomach and replace the stone that had long found a home there.

THREE

Viviann had been awake for hours by the time Peter stirred. She had watched the subtle morning light change the canopy above her from a midnight black to a sea foam blue. The gold stitching that patterned the canopy fabric had kept her mind busy while she waited for Peter to awaken. She reached forty-six stitches, after three rounds of counting, when Peter turned to her, half surprised she was there.

"Hello," Viviann hushed with a light smile, not wanting to interrupt the stillness of the house.

"Good morning," Peter said back, rubbing his eyes. He laid there in an uncomfortable silence for a few moments, and then rose from the bed. He slipped on his dressing robe and out the room. Viviann wasn't sure what to do next, so she laid there a few moments more. She perked up at the slight knock beyond the door, thinking he had come back. Evelyn carried a wide breakfast tray into the room instead and set it on the small table in the bedroom's seating area. The maid still didn't look at her and hurried from the room as quick as she had come.

Every morning was more or less the same. Sometimes she would dress early so she could eat breakfast with Peter, but he would read the paper for the duration of the meal, and she'd be left wishing she had just stayed in bed. Slowly, Viviann got the hang of being a proper lady. Her days were filled with managing the staff; she reviewed menus the cook would come up with for the week, and wrote letters to her mother, trying to ramble as much as possible about the expensive clothes and furniture she was surrounded with. She also spent plenty of time painting and knitting, which she picked up as a last resort to stave off the boredom. Her routine was easy enough: she would awaken and dress in the late morning, spend the afternoon on whatever business she had for the day, take tea in the library, dress for dinner in the evenings, retire to the great room for a late cup of tea afterward, and then lay there while Peter performed his husbandly duty.

At first it had been fast, and Viviann didn't mind it so much once the pain subsided. During the last few nights, however, it seemed to drag on. Did people enjoy this? She heard of women who were "loose with their morals," from her mother's warnings, of course, and wondered if they enjoyed it either. Or were they doing something she wasn't? Her mind often crept to Edward and that helped, but then Peter would be done and roll off her, and she'd be left feeling empty again.

On a stormy day not long after her arrival, Viviann wandered the house. Rain pelted the roof at all hours. Her hometown of Arrosborough was wet, but it was nothing compared to the atmosphere over the Halsby house. Since the wedding, the sky had been a never-ending slideshow of grays, making the house even darker. The servants lit candles during the afternoon in some rooms, but she still found herself squinting through the darkness.

Viviann cradled a basket full of white roses and blue cornflowers, which were still blooming just beyond the front gate. She had watched them dance in the wild rain from the front windows of her bedroom and couldn't resist. She tried to go out there herself, but a footman caught her and insisted on picking them for her, despite her objections. She watched him traipse through the thick mud and rain from the large doorway, feeling foolish. Her parents had plenty of servants when she was a child, although the numbers dwindled as she grew older and her father's gambling problem worsened. Even with their housekeeper and maids, Viviann was still expected to help around the house. She spent many of her younger days toiling in the garden or helping with the laundry. She felt useless as a Lady, with so many people to do everything for her. The footman now kneeled in the mud, as Viviann stood there, wishing she was the one feeling the drops on her face and the wind in her ears.

The flowers' cheery colors were dull in the grey light of the stifling house, but they were alive and fresh, and Viviann felt she could breathe for the first time since she arrived. While she wandered through the corridors and chambers, she placed vases of the bouquets on every surface.

Viviann found an ornate dresser along one of the hallways, housing a strange ceramic elephant (which Viviann guessed was worth more than her family's entire estate) and placed one of the vases next to it. It wasn't the most exciting thing she could've thought of doing, but it helped her ignore the feeling of being watched. Unknown eyes seemed to follow her wherever she went, announcing their presence with ice running up her spine.

A maid rounded the corner from the drawing room where Viviann had placed the previous bouquet. The girl was one of the younger maids, thin and lanky, with perpetually large and empty eyes. In her hands were large piles of dried and dead flowers, faintly white and blue looking.

"Where did you find those?" Viviann demanded before she could stop herself. She saw the poor girl flinch at her words. She rummaged through her mind for the maid's name. She said softer, "Forgive me, Anne. Where did you find those?"

Anne looked down at her hands and shifted on her feet. "They're all over the house, Madame. I'm not sure where they came from."

Viviann dared to come closer to the girl. They were indeed roses and cornflowers. Viviann felt a wave of nausea hit. She glanced around her, trying to spot the bunch she had placed only moments ago.

On the far wall, among a sea of faded wallpaper, sat a vase of dried flowers.

"Did you put these here, your ladyship?" Anne walked to the dead bouquet.

She touched the browning edges of the once fat leaves, which crumbled into dust under her fingertips. Viviann tried to stifle her breathing.

"I just… not even five minutes ago…" she stammered. Before she could finish, the maid collected the flowers and hurried away. The vase still sat in front of Viviann, where murky and spoiled water remained. She hesitated for a moment; she felt the coldness spread from her spine to her neck. She whipped around the hall to see if someone were standing there, thinking maybe Anne hadn't left after all.

There was no one.

Viviann sucked in a deep breath and marched away, shaking. Before she exited the hallway, a shatter rang out from behind her. She whirled around. A figure of an elephant lay in a thousand pieces across the hardwood floors. Viviann crouched to pick up a few wayward shards. The glass was ice cold in her hand. A jagged edge split open her fingertip, and dark blood sprang up from the small cut. She watched it fall to the hardwoods in fat drops, and something beyond the emptiness around her watched as well.

Viviann waited until after dinner to tell Peter about the flowers, away from the ears of Benson, who would probably find a way to blame Anne. He was a pleasant enough man, with an eye for detail and order, but the way he spoke to some of the younger staff could make anyone wince. Viviann feared she had given the girl quite the scare today and didn't want her to be more afraid of her than she already was.

The great room was slowly warming to her, as they spent almost every night here, but on nights like this there was an uneasiness in the air, and there was something ominous about the way the deep red wallpaper glowed in the candlelight. Viviann noticed any evidence of her confusing ordeal earlier had been removed. Peter navigated to a bookshelf, as usual, looking for the book he had started the previous night. Viviann went to pour herself a cup of tea, which was already laid out on the little tea table in front of the sofa.

"Peter, the strangest thing happened today," Viviann began.

Peter found what he was looking for and brought it over to the sofa where she was seated. He raised an eyebrow in reply.

"I tried to place some flowers around the house, but not even an hour later they all seemed to wilt in their vases." It didn't sound quite as alarming as she had hoped. Peter nodded like her story wasn't finished. She was going to mention the shattered elephant, but the words ran dry in her throat.

"It was odd." She said simply. "One minute they were fresh and beautiful, and the next they were dead as if they had been left out for weeks."

Peter contemplated this for a moment. She could tell he was engulfed in a memory by the way he stared off into space, with a soft smile on the edge of his lips. Was it a memory of Elizabeth?

"That is odd. I remember my mother complaining about that once. Actually, she complained about it constantly," he chuckled. "She always thought this house needed fresh flowers."

Viviann was startled by his response. "You never talk about your family."

"I guess I just never know what to say. My father was an extremely quiet man, a little looney towards the end there, and my mother was a very sweet woman. Everyone loved her. I had a younger sister, but she passed when I was eighteen."

Viviann's heart pulled at that. She couldn't imagine anyone saying such a thing about her own mother. She wondered if she had seen his parent's portraits around the house. "What were their names?"

"My father's name was William and my mother's was Ada. She was from Germany. My sister's name was Harriet."

"William? Like your grandfather?" Viviann motioned to the painting hanging above them. William's eyes were darker tonight, with Viviann half expecting them to blink at any moment.

"Great-grandfather, actually. I have memories of my grandfather, but old William here," Peter also motioned to the painting, "he's a man of legend."

There was a sound from upstairs again, quick and sharp, like something had fallen and broken. Or was it a scream? It was too fast to process. Peter didn't seem to notice but Viviann's skin crawled.

The painting's eyes were on her; she could feel them like a hot poker to her back. She needed a distraction, anything, before she ran from the room screaming. She shot up during his story and went to the bar cart across the room. It was one of the best pieces in the house, as it was shaped like a globe, keeping the alcohol and glasses cleverly hidden. She tried to find the latch, but her hands shook so hard she couldn't catch it. She jolted when she felt Peter's hand around hers, helping her finger the latch and open the bar.

"He was mad," Peter said, right in Viviann's ear. "Or at least he was in the end, when my father was born."

Peter stepped back and wandered over to his ancestor's portrait. He leaned against the mantle while Viviann tried pouring a glass of an expensive looking rum. Most of the alcohol splashed across the bar. The scream from upstairs sounded again but clipped. Or was it a creak? Was it the sound of Evelyn walking through her dressing room?

"My father only remembered how he always talked to himself. Things like "I want to go back," that kind of thing. I think my father only told me such things to scare me into bed," he chuckled again.

Viviann gulped the drink down. The taste was strong and sour on her tongue. She couldn't help but make a face when she pulled the glass away.

"He built this house with his own two hands," Peter said, spreading his arms wide to encapsulate everything around them. "Everything we have is thanks to him."

Was that the noise again? Or was it the clink of her long nails on the textured glass in her hands? Viviann wondered. How could Peter not hear it?

"What happened to him then?" Viviann managed to ask between gulps, trying to ignore the noise. The warmth spread through her, and her head already felt foggier. "He built the house, and what? He just turned mad?"

"That, I'm not sure. Apparently, he was some giant East India Company captain. His ship even mutinied against him. Perhaps that is when he went crazy."

The drink was making her fuzzier than Viviann expected. She didn't feel anxious anymore; she just felt tired. Tired down to her bones. The upstairs was quiet.

"If his own ship had mutinied, would they not have killed him?" Viviann wondered aloud. Her eyes drifted to the portrait. Was this imposing figure a great captain of a ship, or just a madman? Viviann tried to imagine him, but her mind came up blank. He was a collection of brushstrokes, that was all. Not real.

"Lord, I hadn't given it a thought. Like I said, he was a legend. More myth than man," Peter answered with a shrug. He gazed up at the painting of William. With the fire dwindling, the shadows grew harsher, and William was cloaked in near darkness.

Viviann was grateful he didn't continue; she had a hard time focusing on the now empty glass she attempted to set down on the bar. She made her way to the door. Peter swirled his drink around but didn't move otherwise, his eyes still glued to William's.

"Are you coming to bed?" Viviann slurred, hoping Peter wouldn't notice.

"No, I think I'll stay here and finish my drink," he said to the painting.

Viviann stumbled up the stairs, to her bedroom, and felt the rush of sleep as soon as her head hit the pillow. She was plagued with dreams filled with fire and the shadowy figure of her true love, and beyond that somewhere, she could hear the rumblings of an angry house.

FOUR

Every morning, Viviann woke with a start. Peter let out a loud snore as she rose from bed and pulled on her robe. She yanked the curtains back as hard as she could, hoping the noise would rouse him from sleep, to no avail. She tugged the cord next to the fireplace, signaling to Evelyn she was up and ready to start her day.

Viviann was becoming used to being dressed by someone else; she held her arms out like a child so Evelyn could slip a dress over her head and pull it down to her waist.

"Is everything alright, my lady?" Evelyn asked while she bent down to slip on Viviann's shoes.

Viviann vaguely heard her. She felt nauseous, which was becoming a daily occurrence. She was surprised that Evelyn spoke at all. She must've noticed that Viviann was giving up her campaign of niceness to befriend her. Viviann was exhausted, in every way she could be, and if Evelyn wanted to be silent day after day, so be it.

The nausea grew worse as the day went on. While Viviann walked through one of the larger hallways between the morning room and her bedroom, she felt the same sensation of being watched as she always did, like an icy finger tracing down her back. Today, however, it was stronger than ever before.

She inspected the dozens of paintings hanging above her, some landscapes, but mostly depicting the same group of people from the rest of the house; a woman with strong features and raven hair, and four younger children. She thought she recognized the woman as William Halsby's wife, Marguerite. The same woman hung side by side to him in the library, but she couldn't be sure. The portraits along the hallway gave her a feeling of deep sadness, as they were all dark and expressionless. Viviann noticed they all had the same forlorn and muddled eyes of everyone else in this house.

One of the larger paintings hung in front of her, some dreary cliffside. Even though there were no figures in the painting, it seemed like she was about to witness someone throwing themselves from it. Maybe that was the point. Maybe she was supposed to see the black of the rocks above the crashing waves and imagine her feet were standing upon it, looking down into the navy sea, feeling the wind on her face as she fell into the treacherous water.

She wanted nothing more than to rip it off the wall. She noticed the light reflecting off the thicker blobs of paint that had been left behind after a brushstroke. She put her hand up to the surface and her fingertips were met with the smooth ridges of wet paint. Navy blue stained her fingers. How could that be? She didn't know of any painters coming by the house and she hadn't heard anything from the servants. Peter had left the house earlier for some meeting in town, but he would've mentioned if he knew anything about it. She might've been out of sorts when she first arrived but by now, she had a handle on the day-to-day workings of the house. She wouldn't have missed something like this.

The house was silent. Not a creak of the floors, not the shuffling steps of someone walking a floor above her. Just, silence.

Another painting, as large as one of the house's windows, dropped from its place on the wall with a loud CRASH, a hair away from Viviann. She jumped back with a loud scream, catching the hem of her gown, and crashing to the ground as well.

She heaved air into her lungs as she stared at the painting's face, which stared back as it leaned on the wall in front of her, dwarfing her. All the times she walked this hallway, she always thought it was a simple painting of the house, on a particularly dark and cloudy night where the moon's absence was heavy on the world. But upon closer inspection, she realized it was a view of the house from the estate's cemetery. A small headstone lay crooked in the corner of the piece. A shadow, really. Or a shadow where a shadow had been. Viviann inched closer, on her hands and knees, to read the writing that was faintly scrawled inside the gravestone.

Viviann Alice Clarke

Viviann gasped at the sight and rubbed her eyes. When she pulled her hands away, the words were gone, but the headstone remained. The background of the ominous house's shadow bore deep into Viviann.

She jumped from her place on the floor and flew down the hallway in the direction of the servant's staircase. Her stomps vibrated the walls around her, but the only sounds she could hear were the swish of her heavy skirts and the blood rushing in her ears. Viviann rubbed the now dried paint between her fingers until little flakes trailed behind her. In the servants' hall, maids were in the corner sewing hems and sleeves, while footmen polished candlesticks with lazy hands. Her heart calmed a little at seeing other people, and she could hear the clambering of pots and pans from the kitchen, as well as Benson's sturdy voice from the back of the house.

Viviann cleared her throat. All the servants jumped like she had caught them in some misdeed, their eyes wide as she stepped further into the room. For a moment everyone was silent. For about the hundredth time since she'd been here, Viviann wondered what Elizabeth was like. Had she ruled the servants with an iron fist?

Evelyn stood up slowly, still holding her needle and thread.

"Did you need me for something, Madame?"

"Is there something so important happening down here that no one could come upstairs when I screamed?"

The servants' faces were mirrors of the same blank expression. How could they not have heard it?

"We didn't hear nothin', M'am. We would've come if we heard," said one of the footmen, Charlie.

"A rather large painting fell off the wall on the second floor, almost crushing me. It rattled the whole goddamn house, it's a wonder none of you heard it."

The servants exchanged glances. They must think I've lost my mind, Viviann thought.

"We'll take care of it, m'am," and off the footman went.

Evelyn lingered for a moment before saying, "Are you hurt, my lady? Do you want me to fetch you something?"

Viviann was shaking underneath the layers of clothing, feeling like her limbs were being set alight from the inside.

"I want someone to tell me what's going on in this bloody house!" She screamed, balling up the fabric of her dress with her fists.

Evelyn was dumbfounded, her hands hovering over Viviann's arm. The rest of the servants stared in shock. Benson ran in but stopped dead in his tracks when he found the source of the noise. Viviann pushed her way from the room before anyone else could speak.

"Tell Mr. Halsby I'll be out for a walk, and to start dinner without me," Viviann called as she dashed up the servant's narrow staircase, holding back tears.

The sun was setting by the time Peter found her, standing at the edge of the property by the cliffside. Viviann hadn't meant to come here, but planned to walk the estate until she grew tired. When she got far enough from the house she felt as if she could breathe again, as if she had decided to go without her corset. When she heard the distant waves on the muddy path, she couldn't help but follow.

It was gorgeous, in a strange way Viviann wasn't used to. Growing up on a farming estate had made her partial to meadow landscapes, where lush green grasses and wildflowers blew in the sun-soaked wind. Where she stood now was the exact opposite of what she had always considered beautiful. Not unlike the painting she studied earlier, patches of weeds gave way to slick flat rock, jutting out from the cliff's edge, all the way down to the water, which looked deep and dark and cold in the fading evening light.

She heard Peter approach but didn't turn to welcome him. She knew they must look so out of place here, her in a lavender afternoon dress and him in his tan suit from earlier. Waves pelted the rocks below, and a wet wind nipped at their faces.

"Benson told me what happened."

Viviann was silent. Her cheeks and eyes were red, but she didn't turn away from the stormy horizon beyond her.

"There is something going on in that house," Viviann said.

Peter sighed. "This is a very old house, dear. Who knows how old that painting is, it's astounding it's stayed up this long."

"I'm not crazy," Viviann murmured, rather flat.

"I never said you were," Peter said, placing a gentle hand on her shoulder, which was tight with deep knots.

"It almost crushed me."

"I know, and I'm glad you're not hurt. I'm having them check the nails on every painting to make sure that never happens again."

Viviann was silent. The wind howled between them and the clouds grew darker.

"Are they hanging it back up?" She finally asked.

"Oh, no, it's gone."

Viviann turned at this.

"It was horrid anyway. Pretty morbid, too."

Viviann choked out a laugh. She finally turned to face him. He was smiling with the same hopeful smile he offered her the day she arrived. His eyes were clearer than they'd been for weeks, like the day she met him. Where was that clarity when they had dinner, or when they followed the same evening routine of retiring to the great room?

"You must be freezing," he said, quickly tearing off his coat and draping it around her shoulders.

She let him envelop her in the thick wool, in his smell. She noticed the pit in her stomach was gone and she had stopped shaking. She let him guide her back to the house.

"Peter," she said while they made their way, his arm around her. "I may have ruined one of the new paintings. I accidentally smudged it before… the whole ordeal. Just tell me when new paintings are being put up around the house so I know to steer clear of it."

"New painting?" Peter said absentmindedly. His arm dropped to his side. "There hasn't been anything new here since my coming-of-age portrait, which had to be ten or eleven years ago."

Later that night, as Evelyn undressed her for bed, Viviann tried to muster an apology. It might not be very lady-like, but the way Evelyn hurried through unpinning her hair, she suspected the girl was more hurt than Viviann first realized.

"Is there anything else, my lady?" Evelyn recited, not even looking at her. She was already walking away by the time Viviann could speak.

"Actually, yes."

Evelyn stopped at the door, her back to Viviann, like a child being scolded.

"I wanted to apologize, for earlier. I...I wasn't myself," Viviann settled on.

Evelyn turned around slowly, compassion drowning her features. "The house… it can do that to you sometimes."

"Things keep happening, and I...," Viviann felt the tears at the back of her throat, tightening her voice.

"It's okay, my lady, really."

"No, it's not okay. I know you're all terrified of me already, I don't want to give you another reason to hate me."

"What? My lady, really, we don't hate you."

"Oh? Is that why you all fall silent the moment I'm around? Or the reason you won't talk to me, even though we spend hours in this bloody room every day?" Viviann shouted. Weeks of being ignored and left feeling stupid was bubbling up to the surface faster than she could stifle it. It was an angry ocean thrashing inside her, crashing into the cliffs that was her skin. She put her face in her hands.

Evelyn walked over. She put a hand on Viviann's back. "Look, my lady, please understand that we're all just a little on edge. We got so used to Lady Elizabeth and then..."

Viviann looked up and used her nightgown to swipe a tear from her eye. Evelyn didn't say anymore, but she kept her hand on Viviann's back. They stayed like that for a while, each one glad for the subtle comfort.

FIVE

The carriage rolled down the estate's drive as Viviann peered through the small window. The grass was shorter, as were most of the other plants that usually swarmed the exterior. After calling the Halsby manor her home for the last few months, looking upon her old house in Arrosborough was quite a shock. It was tiny, but the relief of familiarity felt like a warm hug. Spring's end made the nearby trees an intense green, and their leaves danced along the carriage as they came to a halt.

It had been five months since she slept under this roof. Amazingly, it had been Peter who suggested she go away for a few days. After the painting incident, he thought it best if she spent some time away from the house. Viviann couldn't have been happier. They were sitting across each other at the large dining table, eating a first course of pigeon in white sauce, when he asked whether she was homesick.

"Yes." She surprised herself by how quickly she answered.

Jane and John were standing just outside the door in their best attire, a dress and suit she had never seen before, as if they were expecting the king. Viviann remembered telling her parents Peter was visiting an old colleague in Oxford, but they had dressed on the off chance he was with her. In a weird way she wished he *was* here with her. She wanted to show him where she grew up and the kind of household she was raised in. She wanted him to understand how hard of a transition it was to be married into his house. She tried to hide her frustration with a tight smile, and felt a headache develop at the base of her skull.

"My darling!" Jane exclaimed, throwing her arms out for a bit of drama. Viviann dropped to the gravel before the attendant could help her down. She hugged her mother first, but when she went to hug her father, she felt her mother's eyes on her gown like two hot pokers. Viviann had decided to wear one of her own dresses to her reunion with her parents, even though she had grown quite used to wearing Elizabeth's. Viviann wore a powder blue cotton dress with small white flowers, and a matching hat to complete her ensemble. She looked like the perfect Arrosborough woman, for once in her life.

"I didn't think you'd be in something so informal," Jane couldn't help but say, feigning a laugh.

The comment would've gotten under Viviann's skin had she

not been so excited to be in her old home again. The landscape surrounding the house was bursting with color, tall and stout hollyhocks, fat bundles of lilac, and small forget-me-nots sprinkled across the lush grass. The late afternoon light washed everything in a nostalgic glow, like a fairytale. Viviann wanted to touch every surface and texture she could see, to make sure she was really standing there, her home, like she had never left.

When she crossed the threshold, however, the weight of disappointment lumbered over her. Her parents had changed everything about the entryway, down to the light floral wallpaper that had been replaced with a cherrywood wainscoting, making the small space darker and less inviting. Meanwhile, her parents were floating through the house, eager to show Viviann what she had been missing. They went through to the drawing room after passing the overflowing coat wardrobe. At least some things never change.

The once faded yellow sofas had been replaced with a larger one, one with gold flowers atop a brunt orange background. It was almost as gaudy as the matching, orange-colored carpet beneath their feet.

"Clearly your father and I have made quite a few updates around the house," Jane said with a smirk.

Viviann thought her monthly checks were supposed to be bailing out the estate, not trying to smother it with opulent furniture and fabrics. Her father went to the bar in the far corner of the room and poured himself a drink.

"Where are my paintings?" Viviann asked, noticing the bare walls.

"They're up in your old room."

"You don't want them anymore?"

"Darling, we just put in new wallpaper. They had to go somewhere. We'll get around to hanging them back up, won't we, dear?"

John was busy savoring his sip of sherry. Viviann wasn't a particularly good painter, she knew, and they were displayed for the simple fact that the old wallpaper had been peeling in places. Still, it pained her not to see them on the walls. It had only been a few months. Were they trying to erase her already?

"Tell me, Viviann," Jane said as she pulled Viviann down onto the ugly sofa. "How has married life been? Still lucky and in love?"

"Oh, I guess. It's been nice-"

"Didn't I tell you his estate was gorgeous? Just how big is the house?"

Viviann tallied up the rooms in her head. "Well, there's fifteen guest rooms, if that tells you anything."

"Have you explored much of the garden? I know the weather has just been horrid, but I hear it's one of the largest gardens in Great Britain."

Viviann had to restrain herself from rolling her eyes. It was true, she hadn't spent much time in the gardens, but they weren't that big. The estate was covered in woods, save for the plot that was the house and the drive. Viviann noticed her father finishing his glass.

The conversation stayed on the same trajectory throughout dinner, which was one of her favorites: pork with an apple chutney, served with a large helping of potatoes. Viviann savored the simple flavors, letting their warmth fill her insides to the brim. They hadn't gotten rid of their cook just yet, even though it sounded like they were planning to.

"Our tastes have changed," John shrugged. Whatever that meant.

Later that night, they retired back into the drawing room, where John promptly fell asleep in his chair by the fire. Jane started up her needlework, while Viviann simply twiddled her thumbs at her place on the sofa. With the roaring fire in the small room, Viviann felt warm for the first time in months. In a different life, perhaps, Viviann would be enjoying herself. She would feel welcomed and loved just from being under the slanted roof of her old home and feel equally as grateful to be able to return to her own household the following day. But Viviann did not feel grateful. All she felt was dread. There wasn't room for anything else.

"Mother, can I ask you something?" Viviann, for once, kept her voice empty of attitude. Her mother nodded but didn't turn away from her stitching.

"Did you know Peter was married before?"

Jane put down the needlework and sighed. "Yes, I did."

"Why didn't you tell me?"

"Why would I? It was years ago, darling, it's not like it matters."

"It's just that...all her belongings are still in the house. I wear her old *dresses*, mother."

"Oh? It's really not that unusual, I'm sure lots of new wives do it. It's economical. Besides, a well-crafted dress can be worn for years." Her mother said, wearing a dress that was probably stitched weeks ago while her "well-crafted" dresses lay abandoned in her wardrobe.

Viviann fell silent for a while and picked at her fingertips. She didn't think she'd have the courage to say it, but before she could stop herself, she said, "There's something wrong with the house."

"Is it not in your style? Those old houses are always filled with dusty antiques. You should think about procuring some new pieces. Like what we're sitting on!"

"No, that's not what I mean. There's something *wrong* with the house itself. I feel like I'm being watched wherever I go, and there's always these weird noises coming from upstairs. A few weeks ago, a painting randomly broke and almost crushed me- "

"Viviann, you need to calm down. I'm sure it's not that bad. It's a new place, it's going to feel strange for a while. But I'm sure you *are* being watched."

Viviann perked up at her mother's words. Did she actually believe her?

"Those servants must be watching your every move, waiting for you to make a mistake. You must be careful, Viviann. You may be a proper lady now, but you don't act like it. You must be strict with *those* kinds of people, otherwise they'll walk all over you."

Viviann turned away so she could finally roll her eyes. Their household had six servants while she was growing up; what would her mother know of running a large estate?

"It's just...I can't shake this feeling, mother. I hate it there," Viviann confessed.

"What?" Jane asked sharply, causing her father to grunt in his sleep. "What an awful thing to say. You have more than I could've ever asked for; wealth, a large house, a handsome young man to take care of your every need, for God's sake. Don't be ungrateful."

Viviann just sighed in response. She wasn't naïve enough to think her mother would do something, but she hoped she would at least listen. Viviann looked around at all the unfamiliar furniture in the room and tried to imagine what the place looked like before her wedding. She couldn't.

Later that night, while she lay awake in her small bed, underneath the same rough sheets she had slept under her entire life, Viviann tried to calm her heart enough to sleep. She was safe here, yet her pulse throbbed in her ears. Her room had stayed the same since the day she left, besides the stack of canvases that leaned against the windowsill. Despite the strange new furniture downstairs, she knew every cranny of this house. Every creak in the floorboards, every squeak from a door or cupboard. She heard nothing but the rapid beating of her own heart. Somehow, this still didn't comfort her.

It was many nights after her journey that she was finally able to attain some real sleep. Most of the time, Viviann would lay there wide awake for hours. She could feel the soft linens beneath her, and Peter's warm body at her side. It was almost comforting being like this, with the house completely silent, the safety of the heavy quilts on top of her and her husband mere inches away. In another house, perhaps Viviann would've been fast asleep. But she wasn't, instead she laid on her back shrouded in darkness, icy air biting her nose, and a sense of unease she couldn't shake since the day the painting fell.

The last week had been rough since she had been back. The staff lumbered around, besides Benson and Evelyn -the only two people who seemed to know what they were doing-, and Peter was about as clueless as the rest of them. Viviann kept waiting for something else to happen, but the house was smarter than that, and things had been oddly still.

Viviann found herself in the library one late afternoon. It was a simple rectangle, with the heavy door opening to reveal mahogany bookshelves lining both sides of the room until the fireplace at the other end. She tried not to notice the oval portraits of William and his wife hanging above the mantle. Although the ceilings were high, it wasn't quite two stories. The stacks of books on the floor and overflowing from the shelves made the room feel stifling, and the lack of windows only made it worse. Although it was the middle of May, and the horrid English heat hadn't quite arrived for the summer, she found herself rolling up her sleeves and unbuttoning her collar. The room had been a mess when she found it, after years of neglect. For a man who loved to read, Viviann noted, Peter did a terrible job of taking care of his reading material.

She found a discarded book wedged into the leather chair that sat next to the fireplace. *The Talisman* by Sir Walter Scott. Viviann winced.

It was one of Edward's favorite books. She was instantly transported to the last time she saw him with it, when he was on his deathbed. His once tanned skin was so pale, he looked translucent, and sweat coated his forehead. She asked if he wanted her to read it to him, but he smiled sadly and said "No, I just want to feel it in my hands."

She was in his plain bedroom, for the first and last time. He was wearing just a nightgown and a sheet while she was bundled up tight in her best coat. The nurse that took care of him had opened the windows because his skin was boiling to the touch, but even that wasn't enough.

Viviann inhaled with a pain in her chest, transported back into the Halsby library. Tears blurred her vision, and she crouched on her knees to allow herself a moment to breathe. She felt the soft cover under her fingertips and traced each word of the title. What would Edward think of her now? Of her life here? Would he be happy for her?

She suddenly gripped the book like she was going to rip it in half, her pain turning into rage. She threw it as hard as she could across the room, where it slammed into one of the opposite bookshelves, knocking other books loose with a loud crash.

For a moment she felt better, lighter. The feeling wore off as she realized she would have to clean up the mess she just made. With a sigh, she heaved herself off the floor and made her way to the pile. There was something off about the bookcase she approached, like it was leaning. She tried to straighten it and the entire piece swung open like a door. A rusty creak sounded as she pulled it open in disbelief.

The same mahogany shelves lined the inside compartment. The smell of old dust and rotting wood wafted up to her nose. It was dark in the firelight, and Viviann gingerly felt around at the back of the shelves. When her fingers met something stiff, she ripped her hand away. Nothing scurried beyond the darkness as she stood frozen, so at least it wasn't an animal lurking deep within the shelf. She crouched down and saw a leather book laying perfectly straight on the lower shelf, almost like it had been placed there. It wasn't as dusty as the shelves surrounding it, which was odd for a secret compartment in a strange house. Viviann looked around like the house itself could sense what she was thinking. Everything in the room was still. She heard nothing beyond the crackling fire.

She pulled the book free from a cobweb and opened it as gently as she could. The leather binding cracked as she did so, which was deafening in the silent room.

Inside the cover was the slanted scribbles, *William L. Halsby.*

SIX

The master bedroom was one of the finest bedrooms in the house. It had seafoam green wallpaper with a damask pattern, and dark wood paneling around the fireplace and windows. The room not only contained an impossibly large walnut bed, which was canopied in a fine silk, but a full seating area as well. The tea table and nightstands had marble tops, and an Oriental rug in the same muted colors laid over the plush carpet. That is where she found herself when she started reading William's journal.

When she brought it up from the library, she first tried stashing it under their mattress, dust and all. After laying down that night, she noticed the grime she had tracked on the blankets and sheets, and figured a maid would too. She crept out of bed again and snuck to her dressing room, pulled an old shawl she'd worn in Arrosborough from the depths of some drawer, tucked the journal neatly inside, and placed it deep under her bed. Viviann could think of nothing else for the rest of the day, so she feigned a bad stomachache to excuse herself from dinner. Peter came up to check on her when he returned from his meeting and placed a quick kiss on her forehead. When Evelyn brought a tray of soup to her room, Viviann debated whether she should tell her about her find. She decided she would figure it out once she'd read it, and all but begged Evelyn not to let anyone else disturb her for the rest of the evening.

Finally, Viviann was alone. She stuck her hand under the bed and pulled out the journal. The leather binding made it heavy but there were whole sections that had been ripped out in, what looked like, a fury. Viviann ran her fingertips over the edges of the torn paper, leaving a dark stain wherever she touched. She inspected her hands and realized the grime layering the book wasn't just years of dust like she originally thought. It was ash too, like it had been in a fireplace and partly burned. Did William do it? Did he rip out the pages and then throw it into the fire, only to realize what he had done a second later and pulled it out? She thought of his painting that hung over the fireplace in the great room, but all she could picture were those eyes, flickering from the fire. She turned to the first page.

October 16th, 1750

It is done. After almost a year of waiting, finally it is done.

Where there once was a simple skeleton, just planks of sun-bleached wood laid out on the dirt, there now stands a monster of a house. A castle, almost. Fit for a king. My mind won't recognize it. For months, I've been here almost every day, watching the agonizingly slow progress turn into a living thing, a true home. But when the carriage pulled through the gates today, I still expected to see that vague shape, nothing more than a foundation, a shadow of my father's dream. It was startling to see this three-story manor in its place.

Stranger still, to not see the workers. I can't think about it. What's done is done.

It is no longer "The House," but our house. The place my children will grow old in, where future generations will walk the halls, a perfect line of Halsby's. I would have thought this unfathomable a year ago. So many things have changed.

Marguerite is happy to be out of the inn, but she didn't quite share my enthusiasm when I showed them around today. She still hasn't forgiven me for my unspeakable act. I haven't forgiven myself either. But we're here now. We're lucky we ever made it here. I made sure it was done. It could've been months before it was livable if I hadn't stepped in, years even. But it is done. And there's nothing anyone can do about it now.

March 8th, 1756

Nightmares have plagued me for almost a fortnight. I don't know what else to do. I've tried everything, I roam the grounds like a ghost, trying to tire myself out. I've had all the teas one can try for sleeplessness, and even the doctor gave me some clear liquid to ingest on nights like this. Yet nothing works.

I wake up, drenched in sweat, my heart threatening to leap out of my chest. What's worse is that they feel real, real enough to make me question myself when I'm awake. Even now, is this all just a horrible nightmare? Am I really lying fast asleep -in Paris, perhaps- instead of scribbling at my desk like a madman? I don't know. And I can't dare tell anyone about this. The fact that Marguerite knows I'm not sleeping is bad enough. She's looking for a reason to write to them. So they can take me away again.

The dream is never the same, but it always starts off like this: I'm walking through the house like it was while it was being built, with no furniture and no windows. I end up wandering around until I find a room with one of the children in it or Marguerite. Suddenly all the furniture is back but there's a sense of something not being right. The children and Marguerite never turn around, even when I call to them. Usually, I end up reaching for them but when my hands make contact, they disintegrate into a pile of bones and empty clothing. I end up running out of the room, calling for help. Tonight, as I dashed to the staircase, they started crumbling underneath my feet, splitting open to reveal nothing but a black void below. I fell, and then I was awake, in my bed again. Except I wasn't. Something still felt wrong. When I looked to the side of me, Marguerite was there with a knife, ready to slash at me. Then I truly awoke.

I saw Marguerite to the side of me and she was peacefully asleep. I couldn't calm myself down though, so I came to my study, figuring writing would help.

Has it? Not really. I still feel as jumpy as I was when I woke, and even the fire crackling behind me has been enough to startle me, convincing me someone is in the room with me. I don't know how much more of this I can take.

March 19th, 1756

Last night's dream was one of the worst. I say dream instead of nightmare because I didn't wake up abruptly like I usually do, I woke to Marguerite rising from bed. It was barely morning, just after. I had slept through the night. But I didn't feel rested.

I dreamt of Jonathon.

I found him in the drawing room, playing with a set of trains he had back in France. I was scared to touch him, but I couldn't help myself. It's been six years. You'd think I would've forgotten how he felt, what he smelled like. But when my hand touched his shoulder, I felt him. He stopped playing and slightly turned. I thought I would finally be able to see his face.

But he dropped to the ground, as himself this time, looking like he did the day of the accident. Blood all over his face and clothes. I held him in my arms, just like I had that day, and suddenly I could feel Marguerite next to me, sliding out from the blankets.

I didn't have trouble discerning whether my wakefulness was real or not. The heaviness in my chest reminded me just how awake I really was.

My son. My boy. What have I done?

April 19th, 1758

I am reminded of the good still in the world. For the first time in months, Marguerite and I made love. I had long given up hope that we might rekindle things after Jonathon, but last night we just looked at each other and that was that. It was so good just to hold her again, like I used to, with her looking at me like she used to. It was dawn before we finally went to sleep.

Now, I sit in the gardens with Josephine. She is quite the artist, already. Amelia is due any day now, the doctor said, which will hopefully mean the welcome of my first grandson in the next few days. The first of many, I hope. James told me at breakfast today the name of the baby if it is to be a boy -William. Even with everything that's happened, he still thinks my name worthy of his son.

I feel content. These last few years made me think I didn't even know the word. Right now, I feel like my heart could burst with happiness.

June 3rd, 1758

That selfish, spiteful bitch! She's turned the children against me. I know she did. James asked me what happened to Jonathon today. Why would he ask me such a thing? I didn't know what to say so I lied, thinking I could spare him. Marguerite had already told him! When he wouldn't speak to me in the next few days, Marie finally told me the truth. Marguerite had told them everything. Now James won't speak to me. He won't even look at me. He's threatened to take William away from the house and raise him elsewhere.

Marie thinks he's just grieving for Amelia, since it has only been a week since the burial. He was serious, though, I could see it in his eyes. How could she do this to me? After everything I've given her. After everything I've done for us.

I knew I couldn't trust her. I knew something like this would happen! How could I be so stupid? Why did we even come here? Oh God, please forgive me. I know not what to do. Give me strength, give me peace, SOMETHING. I can't keep doing this. I can't live like this. My boy, my beautiful boy, gone. Just like that. What is wrong with me? I can't work, I can't sleep, I can't THINK. All I see is his face. His beautiful face, gone. Skin dripping off of bone, his eyes looking in opposite directions and spewing blood, his clothes red red red with his blood.

What is happening to me?

June 5th, 1758

What have I done? What have I done? What have I done?

What's wrong with me? I didn't know what else to do. They know. How could they not know? The children know, they must. How can I face them? I feel as if my heart will give out. I wish it would. Perhaps then I shall be cleansed of my sins.

That was it. The next few pages were blank and then just the charred remains of the back cover. Viviann went back to the first page and noticed the date. There didn't seem to be any missing pages in the beginning of the journal. Where did this loose page come from then? It was in the same scrawl, if a bit tighter. It didn't look like the page had been torn out either; it had a perfect edge, like the binding had broken and let all the pages loose. She reclined into bed, reeling. She had forgotten where she was for a moment. The house was unbelievably quiet.

She felt much too restless to sit anymore so she got up and started pacing. She wrapped up the journal and slid it back under the bed, just in case.

She tried to piece together what she had just read. She remembered what Peter had said about him. William was crazy. He certainly seemed crazy by the last few entries, but the first one? He just seemed deeply alone and sad. What had happened to his son, Jonathon? Viviann could only imagine the terrible. A sick feeling had settled in her stomach while she was reading, but below that her curiosity was taking over. She needed to know more, and it was clear she wasn't going to find it in the journal.

At first, Viviann didn't know what to do. She fell into a restless sleep and didn't wake when Peter got into bed or when he left the next morning. When she awoke, Viviann felt an answer tug at the back of her mind. She jumped out of bed. She went to the fireplace across the room and pulled the cord for Evelyn.

She began digging through her dressing room for a proper day dress and mapped out the beginnings of her plan. She had to know more about this house. This strange family.

"I'm going into town," Viviann called to Evelyn when she heard her enter. She was busy trying to clasp a modest burgundy dress from the back, her arms contorting to manage the small buttons.

"You're what?" Evelyn choked, rushing over to help her. "Are you feeling better?"

"Yes, and I'm going into town. I have some business to take care of. But first, I need you to tell me where I can find Doctor Salinger, and Andrew Bradley," Viviann recited. Peter had written their names out for her, in case of emergencies, which she kept folded in her desk.

"Dr. Salinger, my lady? But you just said you were feeling better."

"I am feeling better. This is for a different matter."

Evelyn raised an eyebrow and looked like she was going to fight Viviann on the issue. She didn't. Instead, she asked, "Andrew Bradley, the lawyer?"

"Yes. And would you, by chance, know where Lord Halsby is this morning?"

"Yes, my lady, he went riding right after breakfast. He said he wouldn't be back for a few hours."

"Perfect."

SEVEN

Thanks to Evelyn, Viviann now stood in the middle of Halsbrook for the first time since her wedding. It was a bustling little city, crowded with modest stone shops and cobblestone streets, where people were swarming over cart vendors selling sweets or flowers. The afternoon sun streamed through thick clouds to cast a soft glow over everything.

Viviann felt invigorated. The journey was longer than she expected it to be, and her bottom half ached from sitting for so long. The winding from the estate made her stomach nervous. Now that she was out of the carriage, she felt her insides settle. It was a vastly different town then when she stayed here for her wedding. It was brighter, full of life and activity. The town was quite lovely with its small river that ran right through the center of it. How had she not noticed before? The air was lighter here; easier to breathe, despite the chill. She thought of how little she knew about this town, about her own husband, in fact. No one in Arrosborough had heard of Peter Halsby before her father had introduced him.

On her journey, she passed a handful of larger homes a few miles from the Halsby estate, homes belonging to Halsbrook's wealthy families, she didn't doubt. They didn't exhibit the same strangeness as the Halsby Manor did. Beautiful flowers sprouted throughout the lawns and gardens of their "neighbors," and Viviann wondered what it would've been like had she married into one of those households instead.

She straightened her overcoat and smoothed down her skirts. She was here for some answers.

The carriage had pulled up to the dress shop, which was her guise for going out. She told the carriage boy, who was attending her, she would meet him in a few hours and sent him on his way. Evelyn helped with providing him a list of items the household needed, which would allow Viviann to wander off on her own while he shopped.

There was a rack of dresses outside the shop, which Viviann sifted through without really looking. She noticed a few townspeople looking at her while they passed, whispering. Just as Viviann turned to carry on past the shop, she crashed into an older woman wearing a starched working dress and apron.

"Lady Elizabeth?" The woman asked incredulously, pale as a ghost.

Viviann didn't know what to say. She was wearing one of her dresses, so it made sense. But the woman had been startled by her face, not just her attire. Viviann heard the carriage finally continue down the street. The woman was still looking at her, and some other pedestrians stopped to look as well.

"No...I'm sorry, there's been a mistake" was all Viviann managed before hurrying past the older woman, towards Halsbrook's small hospital, all the while trying her best to set her jaw and keep her head high.

"I don't think I quite understand the meaning of your visit, Lady Halsby," Dr. Salinger said. "You said you're feeling alright?"

"Oh, yes. I didn't come here for me."

Dr. Salinger led Viviann to his office and guided her inside. It was a large room, with ornate furniture suitable for a hospital's head doctor. A small window close by was opened a jar, allowing a chilling breeze to flutter the mess of papers on his desk. He motioned to the plush chair that sat in front, which Viviann accepted. He seemed alarmed at her statement, but only for a second, as his nervous glance quickly turned to a confident smile.

"So, what can I help you with today, my lady?"

"Dr. Salinger, I understand that you must keep a detailed record of all the patients you see, whether they come to the hospital or you visit them at home. I imagine that all doctors like yourself would keep similar records. Am I correct?"

"Certainly."

"Is it safe to assume, then, that those records could be traced back many years to particular patients?"

"Lady Halsby, what are you saying?" Dr. Salinger's forehead started to sweat.

Viviann clasped her hands together. "I'm looking for the medical records of the Halsby family."

As Viviann suspected, he was stunned. "For what purpose?"

"Doctor, I am new here, and I'm simply curious to know my new family better."

"Well, what exactly do you want to know?" He stammered. "Are you having difficulty falling pregnant?"

It was Viviann's turn to be stunned. She was ashamed to say it, but she had never really given any thought to pregnancy until he said the word. She felt her cheeks burn but continued anyway.

"No, I was hoping to understand what ailments the Halsby line has suffered. I'm aware of the rumors," she added. She didn't know any but she figured a strange family such as the Halsby's had to have a few rumors circulating.

Dr. Salinger seemed to tense slightly at this, but proceeded to the large bookshelf behind him, where many leather-bound books sat with names and years scribbled on the spines. He opened the window wider. "I inherited some records from previous doctors that have practiced medicine here, but I can't promise you they'll have what you're looking for."

"Let's start with Harriet Halsby, Lord Halsby's sister," Viviann said.

"Ah, yes, Lady Harriet," Salinger said as he pulled a book from the shelf by memory. "I was her doctor at the time. She suffered from hysteria, among other things."

"What other things, exactly?"

"Delusions mostly, as well as an acute case of melancholy." He rifled through the book until he came to the page he was looking for.

"Does that mean she killed herself?"

Salinger jumped at the harsh words but continued through the page. "No, like I said, it was hysteria."

"How does one die of hysteria, doctor?" Viviann asked, trying to manage her tone. "I'm sorry, medicine is not something I'm the least bit familiar with."

Salinger smiled with condescension. "Hysteria is essentially a fever of the brain. It can make the sufferer believe they are in constant peril. Obviously, this can wear down the body and mind significantly, until one day the body can no longer sustain itself. If it's quite severe, like it was in Lady Harriet's case, it can lead to death."

"Are you saying she was scared to death?" Viviann said, chewing through the thought in her mind.

"It's not quite that simple, but I suppose you could think about it like that. Very tragic."

"What about anyone else in the family? Any other *tragic* deaths?" Viviann asked.

Salinger gave her a nervous smile before he shelved the book he had been reading from. "The only other tragic death involving the

Halsby's was Lord Halsby's first wife, Lady Elizabeth."

Viviann nodded, still trying to forget the woman's comment about her earlier. Her hands began to sweat inside her gloves. "Are you sure that's it? It's very important to me that I know all the facts, doctor."

"Well, there were the sad cases of Lord Halsby's father, William, and his uncle, Charles. They were taken to the sanitorium, I'm afraid."

Interesting, Viviann thought. Three mad family members. That didn't look good for William. The doctor stood up, clearly hoping Viviann would take the hint and make her exit. She remained seated.

"How far back do your records go? I'm curious what happened to the original Halsby's. I understand their names were William and Marguerite."

"Unfortunately, our records go back as early as 1790."

"Really?" Viviann stood up and walked around Salinger's desk. He seemed appalled but said nothing. She pointed to a journal on the top shelf, the leather cracking from age. "This one says 1750."

Sweat was really starting to pool on Salinger's forehead. He nervously yanked out his handkerchief and blotted it across the spans of wet space. "Ah, yes, thank you, Lady Halsby. I fear my mind has lost its sharpness with age."

He pulled it out. The pages were stiff and almost translucent, with ink that was so light you could hardly see it. Viviann wanted to rip it out of his hands.

"Ah, here it is." Dr. Salinger paused for a moment. "Marguerite Halsby was found strangled in bed in May of 1758. William killed himself shortly after."

Uncomfortable silence filled the room while she digested the information.

"How did he kill himself; did it say?" Viviann finally asked.

"Really, Lady Halsby." He was closing the book and inching away from her. "I'm not sure what you mean to- "

"Dr. Salinger, please," Viviann said with a stern look, channeling her mother.

It seemed to have worked as he opened the book again. He sighed. "He was found to have buried himself in a shallow grave. He suffocated."

The image of William breathing in mouthfuls of dirt wouldn't leave Viviann's head, even as she sat in the office of Andrew Bradley. He was much more relaxed by her curiosity than the doctor had been, and even offered to show her some ledgers he knew belonged to a previous Halsby lawyer.

"I appreciate you helping me understand my new family," Viviann said when he came back in, holding several thick books and folders.

"Of course. I'm surprised you didn't come earlier. I think it's important for a woman to know about the household she's married into. What exactly can I help you with?"

"I'm curious as to the mysterious deaths on the property."

Andrew didn't look the least bit surprised. He simply nodded and looked through the folders. He offered her what he had decided was the right one. "Ah, yes. A hefty sum of the Halsby fortune has gone to settlements. Has something new happened?"

Viviann looked through the files. Most of it was gibberish but she saw distinct figures with names.

Mary Norrwea – 1,000 pounds for the death of her son, Philip Norrwea

John Taffer – 1,000 pounds for the death of his mother, Erica Taffer

Sarah Daniels – 1,000 pounds for the death of her daughter, Sophie Daniels

"I don't understand," Viviann said. "None of these are Halsby's."

Finally, Andrew looked surprised. "Oh, I'm sorry, I guess I misunderstood you. I thought you were looking for the settlement papers the Halsby's have filed, for the lawsuits against the family."

"Lawsuits? So, these were all paid because someone died on the property?"

"Yes. Erica Taffer was said to be the mistress of William Halsby Jr., Lord Halsby's father, although I try not to listen to gossip. The doctor ruled her death an accident, but her son was convinced otherwise. We were forced to settle."

Viviann was shocked. "And the others?"

"The others were servants. Mostly children, unfortunately."

"So, what is all that?" Viviann asked, pointing to the other folders and books littering his desk. All of them had *Halsby* across the spine, painted in gold. A wave of nausea washed over her, and the papers felt impossibly heavy in her hands.

"These are all the records of what the estate pays for, broken down month to month. And this," he grabbed a smaller notebook. "This is a list of the sources of money for the estate. It's stayed more or less the same for the last hundred years. You're welcome to take any of these if you need. Everything's been copied already, and these are just the reserves. We learned our lesson after Lady Elizabeth," the lawyer chuckled.

"Lady Elizabeth came here?"

"Yes, a few weeks after her marriage to Lord Halsby. She came in many times to look all this over, which is why we started copying it."

When Viviann left the small office, she felt almost feverish, and the bright sun was only making it worse. One of Bradley's clerks followed her until she found her carriage, where he unloaded a crate of the records onto the seat across from her. Viviann was stupefied, her brain rattling with all the concerning information it had just absorbed.

"Back to the house, m'am?" The small carriage boy called to her from the front. He seemed so young. She wondered if the other servant children who had died had been around his age.

For a second, she wondered about telling him differently; telling him to take her as far as Arrosborough so she could abandon this place. But what after that? Stay with her parents? There was obviously no place for her there anymore. Out of the question.

"Yes, thank you," Viviann settled on. The carriage beneath her rolled forward and started the long, winding journey back to the house.

EIGHT

A few days after her visit to the doctor and lawyer, and after countless hours of rifling through the ledgers and William's journal, Viviann wandered the house trying to collect her thoughts. It was a gray morning, like any other, that turned into a dark afternoon, the sky thick with clouds, heavy with icy rain. Every inch of the house was covered in candles, yet Viviann still found herself stumbling around in the near dark on the third floor. She hadn't been up there since the tour on her wedding day. It was like the second floor, with the same-colored wallpaper stretching through the hallways and the same carpet lining the floors. Paintings covered every inch of wall space, and

Viviann spent most of her time guessing who was in each portrait.

Something didn't add up in William's journals. For starters, half of the pages were missing. And she still didn't know what happened to his son, Jonathon. Something awful, Viviann knew. Was that what turned him mad? Viviann doubted the journal hiding under her bed was the only journal William kept throughout his life. There had to be more. If there was a secret compartment in the library, there had to be more scattered throughout the house. Viviann wandered through the guest rooms, thinking of places these secret compartments could be. Peter's study was an obvious place, but Peter had been buried in his office since the weather turned bad, so doing any form of snooping was out of the question. Viviann tried to emulate William's mindset. If she were him, where would she have built one? Something told her to go to the third floor. For such a large house that rarely saw any guests, there were dozens of extra bedrooms. She thought it sounded like the perfect place to start her search.

She went to any form of shelving unit in the rooms first and tugged on the shelves or frame until she heard the furniture creak under her strain. Next, she checked the fireplaces. Viviann was in the yellow guest room, at the far corner of the house. A beautiful painting depicting daisies in a yellow vase hung on the wall over the small stone fireplace. She immediately felt like she recognized the painting when she saw it, even though she was convinced she had never stepped foot into this room before. She came closer and saw a sloppy *JH* in the corner, in dark blue paint. She studied the vase and realized she had seen it before, during her flower fiasco what seemed like a lifetime ago. Whoever JH was, they had depicted the vase's iridescent quality perfectly.

She started tracing the painting's frame, seeing if there was some sort of button or knob. She even took the piece from the wall, only to reveal a brighter square of yellow flowered wallpaper. It was heavier than it looked, and she doubted she would be able to lift it again. She left it leaning on the wall while she continued her search. The fireplace was small and dirty, which was strange since it must've been months before someone had used it. Taking this as a clue, she crouched onto her knees and felt inside the fireplace's mouth.

There was a distinct creak behind her, like a floorboard under someone's foot. Viviann's breath caught, and she sat frozen with fear, her hand still inside the fireplace and black with ash. She gathered the courage and turned sharply. The room was empty. The door was a jar, however, and Viviann couldn't be sure she had left it open.

She rose to her feet and wiped her soot covered hand on the skirt of her navy dress, still leaving a noticeable stain behind despite the gown's dark color. Viviann approached the door while holding her breath, trying to keep her footsteps light. She swung the door open with an intense squeak, jumping into the hallway to discover whatever was hiding there. There was nothing. The corridor was long and lined with heavy doors. There was no way someone could've slipped into one of the other guest rooms so silently. She was sure she heard something though. Viviann looked back into the yellow room.

There was something dark on the wall across the room. It was little more than a shadow. As Viviann got closer she realized it was a dirty handprint. She inspected her own hand, but there was barely any ash left on it; not enough to leave a full print. Viviann knew the house was playing some trick on her. She closed her eyes so she could better listen to the creaking of the house. There was none. Perfect silence. Viviann opened her eyes and was surprised to still see the handprint there. It looked so real. Before she could stop herself, she reached out to compare the size of her own hand to the handprint. If her fingers were more slender, it would've been a perfect match.

A hand jutted out from the yellow wallpaper, like it was made of the wallpaper itself. It gripped Viviann's wrist with the heat of a hot poker, sizzling Viviann's skin. She let out a scream before she tore her hand away, stumbling backward and tripping over her dress. By the time she got up and looked back at the hand, there were six more, darting through the wallpaper and reaching out to her like they would gouge her eyes out if she were closer.

Viviann pulled up her skirts and ran from the room as hard as she could. She could hear the fast creaks of her footsteps, but then realized there were more, like a stampede was rushing behind her. She casted a glance over her shoulder but saw nothing. As she turned around, a door swung open. Viviann slammed into it with enough force to bend the door back on its hinges. The door struck her right in the center of her forehead, and she blindly fell to her knees and then onto her back.

Footsteps were approaching from somewhere, but she could hardly see. Her brain throbbed against the lining of her skull, and she tasted coppery blood on her lips. Viviann stopped fighting and gave into the pain and darkness that filled her.

NINE

Flashes of light exploded beyond Viviann's eyelids. She could see Peter, his face and hands distorted as he leaned over her. Her vision blurred and she saw more fragments of light, wallpaper patterns, ceiling tiles, and even some of the servant's faces. Dull pain radiated throughout her body, but she couldn't pinpoint it. She couldn't pinpoint anything.

She woke with a start, gasping air through her worn out lungs. She was in her bedroom, wearing a pale blue nightgown, one she brought from Arrosborough. The soft fabric was comforting between her fingers. She noticed Evelyn reading in the corner. When Viviann stirred, Evelyn threw down her book and ran from the room.

It was light outside, and it took Viviann a moment to realize why she was there. When the realization hit, she tore at her nightgown's sleeves. There was a deep red mark on her wrist where the hand had grabbed her, but it didn't exactly look like a burn. She wrapped a protective hand over the angry flesh. Hunger bloomed in her stomach, as ferocious as a beast. Somewhere beyond the walls she heard voices, growing louder as they neared her room.

Dr. Salinger entered first; his large stomach barely contained beneath his coat buttons. He looked different than the last time she saw him. His singular tuff of silver hair stood wildly atop his head, making his whole appearance messy. He looked nervous; he scanned the room as if he expected an attacker to be lurking in every corner. Peter entered next and sighed with relief at seeing her sitting up and awake.

With her hands hidden under the covers, Viviann traced her fingers over the familiar material of her sleepwear and took some even breaths.

"Hello, Lady Halsby. You suffered quite a nasty fall yesterday."

"Yesterday?" Viviann croaked.

Dr. Salinger's nervous eyes glanced around the room again while she spoke. "Yes, Madame. It seems like you hit your head on one of the guest room doors, upstairs. Fairly hard, I'm afraid. Do you know what happened that might have caused it?"

Viviann was aware of everyone staring at her, and she instinctively brought her hands to her face. When her fingers brushed her nose, she winced. It was swollen and tender, as was the area beneath her eyes.

"Do you remember anything before the accident?"

Viviann almost laughed at the word. *Accident.* They were waiting with bated breath, but she didn't know what to say. Would they think she was mad if she told them the truth? With the doctor's fidgeting, she wondered if he felt the unease in the house like she did. She took a chance.

"I saw something, or I thought I saw something, and when I ran down the hallway to get away, a door suddenly opened, and I crashed into it. I don't remember anything else."

"Saw what, darling?" Peter pleaded. The doctor's discomfort quickly morphed into nail biting. Not a sound could be heard throughout the house.

"I saw something in the wall. Upstairs, in the yellow guest room. There were these hands, clawing at me. I was terrified, so I ran."

The company surrounding her was silent.

"One of them grabbed me, and even burned me." She finally held her wrist out. Evelyn stifled a gasp at the sight.

The doctor immediately took her arm and began inspecting the mark, turning her wrist over many times. Peter looked horrified, and frozen. Dr. Salinger released Viviann's hand and sat at the edge of the bed.

"You said something burned you? That's not a burn, my lady, it looks like nothing more than a bruise. Are you sure you didn't acquire it during the fall? Perhaps you hit it against the door?"

"Well, it felt like a burn; at least, I think. And it *was* a hand. Coming from the wall."

Dr. Salinger exchanged a dubious look with Peter, who rubbed the center of his forehead and sighed in exhaustion.

"You think a hand came out of the wall in the upstairs guest room? For God's sake, Viviann. Do you know how mad you sound?"

"Peter, I know what I saw-"

"How do you know what you saw? Look at your face, darling!" Peter roared. "I'm astonished you even know your own name right now."

"He's right, Lady Halsby," the doctor said, rising. "With the amount of bruising, it's expected to experience some confusion."

Peter stormed to the floor to ceiling windows across the room. Tiny rain droplets were collecting on the glass.

"Lady Halsby, from now on you must be more careful, take better care of yourself. Any form of trauma to your body or mind, or experiencing high levels of stress," he turned to look at Peter, "is not good for your condition."

"What?" Viviann and Peter said at the same time.

"It seems you are with child, your ladyship."

Peter turned to look at her, his anger melting in an instant. There was a half-smile on his face, and Viviann felt the pressure of tears build behind her eyes.

"You were lucky this time, Madame. I wouldn't put yourself at risk again."

With that, the doctor bowed to Viviann, shook Peter's hand, and left the room.

"This is wonderful news, darling. Just wonderful." Peter floated over to her to deliver a quick kiss, which she could hardly reciprocate. A throbbing headache erupted behind her eye sockets. "I'll write to Bradley straight away. We have an heir now."

Before she could even register what he had said, he left the room as well, leaving Evelyn looking stunned in the corner.

"Do you need anything, Madame?" her small voice called. She was edging closer and closer to the door, like she too wanted to sprint away from her.

"Just something to eat, thank you."

When the maid was gone, and Viviann was finally alone, she got out of bed and made her way to the large decorative mirror that stood between two windows. Her arms and legs were stiff, and her joints ached like she had been trapped in a coffin for months. It was another rainy day, to no one's surprise, but there was just enough light to illuminate her figure. When she finally saw her full reflection, she had to stifle a scream. She could tell from everyone's faces that her injuries were bad, but she didn't expect them to be *this* bad. It didn't look real. She brought her shaking fingertips to her face to confirm that it was truly her. The dim lighting made her messy blond hair look white, and the thin blue nightgown made her skin look equally as translucent. She was but a ghost. A banshee.

She let the tears come. They were silent at first, calmly rolling down her cheeks, and Viviann tried to convince herself they were tears of joy. Weren't all women happy when they found out they were going to be mothers? Viviann felt her stomach, realizing she had a significant amount of bloat. Her tears soon turned into sobs; she fell to her knees and gripped the mirror's hazy surface to keep from crying out. Pain pulsated from her face down to her body in waves. How could she possibly raise a child like this? Here, of all places?

TEN

Viviann's life seemed to change overnight. She no longer wore a corset, for one, and was forced to eat breakfast in bed, per Peter's insistence. Servants checked on her every hour, sometimes just peaking their heads around the corner to locate her before running off. Everyone treated her like an invalid, or worse, like she was a child. Peter was the worst of them all. Anytime they were together he would make comments about her condition. He would constantly feel her stomach, as if he could feel the baby through the layers of her skin. Viviann was sick of it. All her pregnancy did for her was make her more on edge. Her face was slowly healing, which meant it grew worse before it started to fade. Everyone in the house, including Viviann, tried to ignore it at all costs. The servants wouldn't look at her, and even Peter would avert his eyes if she turned around too quickly. The dark purple stain spread across the bridge of her nose and settled underneath her eyes. Her nose was still inflamed, but it was a miracle it wasn't broken.

After a fortnight, the purple began to fade into a deep yellow. A few darker marks lingered across her face, but Dr. Salinger assured her it was all part of the healing process. Even still, she asked the servants to remove the mirrors from her bedroom and any of the common rooms, not wanting to risk even catching a glance.

It was easy to elude Peter in the afternoons when he would be holed up in his study or wandering the grounds, but it was next to impossible after dinner, when they would retire into the great room. Viviann couldn't stand to see the painting of William anymore. Not after what happened. There were a handful of others throughout the house she couldn't avoid already. She usually made an excuse of being tired or even feeling sick so she could steer clear of the room entirely.

"Before we go through, I have something to tell you, darling," Peter said one evening while they still sat at the large oak dining table. The dual fireplaces on opposite sides of the room casted conflicting shadows across their faces.

Tonight, of all nights, Viviann actually did feel sick. The combination of their rare steak meal with the deep red wallpaper surrounding them, made her feel like she was draped in blood. She was even convinced she could smell it. Bile rose in her throat.

"I decided we're going to invite everyone we know to a ball, to celebrate our wonderful news," Peter looked as proud as ever. He leaned back in his chair, smiling, asking with his excited eyes for a happy response. He actually looked at her this time.

"A ball?" was all Viviann managed.

"Yes! We should've done something right after the wedding but better now than never. It would also give you a chance to meet our neighbors properly. There are quite a few families with small fortunes in Halsbrook, which means quite a few wives to befriend."

Wonderful, Viviann mused. She wondered if they were as snobby as the gentry in Arrosborough. On the other hand, though, the prospect of being around other people excited her. She was tired of being invisible to everyone outside the house.

"What do you think?" He asked.

She grazed the last bit of tender flesh on her cheek, feeling more like herself since the accident. "That would be lovely, actually."

It took a week for Viviann to receive responses to the Halsby's invitation. Usually, this was a task delegated to her mother, and Viviann wrote the letters with pride. A smile rested on her lips, and she felt more at ease than she ever had. The house couldn't possibly harm her with so many people around. There were only eight larger households in Halsbrook, so much for "everyone they knew," so she decided to send some invitations to her old contacts in Arrosborough; not that she thought they would come.

Viviann was in the morning room at her desk, still one of her favorite places to be, as it was the brightest room in the house.

Yellow wallpaper lined the upper half of the walls, while white wood framing decorated the bottom portion. A tufted, cream-colored sofa sat in the middle of the room, with gold accents in the stitching and legs of the piece. It was a grand version of the guest room upstairs. Viviann tried to ignore the thought.

Although it was early afternoon, and the sun was already peering through the oak's leaves, Viviann kept turning around to look out the window, as if she expected someone to be standing there. The house had been quiet since her little "incident," which only unsettled Viviann more. The hairs on the back of her neck never ceased to be standing at attention. The extreme fluctuations in temperature were still present throughout the rooms, but nothing more concrete. Just as Viviann was about to look over her shoulder again, she caught the last lines of a letter she was holding.

Despite its past, we understand the Halsby Estate to be quite an example of architectural superiority and gentile excellence. My husband and I would be much obliged to join you on the evening of the 26th. We are greatly looking forward to it.

Despite its past? What did that mean? Did she mean Elizabeth? She couldn't imagine the family would've told anyone the details of Elizabeth's death. Viviann checked the envelope and noted it was from an Eleanor Wadsworth. She placed it in the pile with the rest of the responses but couldn't look away from it. She cursed the spark of curiosity that was growing inside her. Her face was still sore, and the memory of what she saw that day was sharp at the back of her mind. Viviann got up and pulled the bell cord for an attendant.

Before long, her and Evelyn were huddled in her dressing room; Evelyn's eyes were as wide as saucers.

"Really, my lady, I have no idea," Evelyn said for the fourth time.

Viviann sighed and plopped down in the vanity's chair.

"We should probably start the alterations for your ball gown," Evelyn mumbled. "Have you picked a dress?"

Viviann perked up slightly. Viviann had found her favorite dress from Arrosborough in the back of the armoire. It was one of the most luxurious she had owned before marrying Peter; the coral silk still had an iridescent shine to it, but she knew it would look like a day dress compared to all the other women at the ball. Evelyn would embellish it so the short sleeves were puffier, and the skirt was larger, as well as add an inch to the waist to make up for the slight bump of Viviann's stomach, which she was glad to cover.

After a long stretch of silence, Evelyn confessed, "I really don't know much, my lady. Rumors. Probably all untrue." She was pinning extra fabric to the bottom portion of the gown that now wrapped Viviann's figure. The blankets that once covered the dressing room's mirrors now lay discarded on the floor. Viviann watched Evelyn's shaky hands slip pins into the excess fabric, catching her thumb more than once.

"Rumors tend to be more true than people realize," Viviann offered, remembering the "rumors" surrounding her father on his gambling habits. "Please, I just need something. I feel like I'm going mad."

Evelyn sighed. "You're not mad, my lady. All I know is that everyone says the family is cursed."

"Cursed?"

"Lady Elizabeth's death was, obviously, quite a shock to us all, but a lot of the servants and the people in town weren't surprised. They said it was just part of the curse."

Viviann thought about Mrs. Wadsworth's letter. *Despite its past.*

"That's why no one in Halsbrook wanted to marry Lord Halsby. Lady Elizabeth's death convinced everyone the curse was true."

Viviann was surprised how much that information hurt. Not that it didn't make sense; Viviann had long puzzled why Peter had come all the way to Arrosborough to get a wife. It wasn't like she thought her good looks and quick wit won her the name of Halsbrook's richest inhabitant.

"What about before that?"

"Well, there was Lady Harriet, who died about ten years ago. I was just a young housemaid then, so I had almost no interaction with her."

"What do you remember?"

"They said it was hysteria. They found her in a wardrobe."

Evelyn finally looked up and met Viviann's wide eyes. They had been whispering, like they were discussing something secret and the very walls would hear them. They were probably right.

"Do you think that's really what happened to her?"

Evelyn took a step back, eyeing the temporary adjustments she had made. Viviann looked down and was surprised to see her skirt almost twice as full, with pinned gigot sleeves that swallowed her upper arms in silk. She looked into the mirror she had been avoiding while Evelyn worked, and noticed she looked quite pretty. The markings on her face were so light she could hardly see them, and the rosy color of the bodice washed her skin in a healthy glow. For a moment, she forgot she was pregnant. She looked like herself. Her old self.

"I don't know what to think anymore." Evelyn said. She carefully undressed Viviann and helped her into a somber sapphire gown for that night's dinner.

"Do you miss her? Lady Elizabeth, I mean."

"Yes." Evelyn said without hesitation. "I didn't have anyone growing up. I was in an orphanage until I was old enough to work, then I came here. Elizabeth was my first *real* friend."

Evelyn's eyes grew glassy and she turned away from her, fidgeting with something on the vanity table. Viviann noted how Evelyn had left out the word "lady" this time. When was the last time someone called her by her own name? *Just* her name?

"There is something, though, that I think you should see." Evelyn was looking at her through the vanity's mirror, her eyes now dry.

She slipped out of the room for a few minutes, leaving Viviann to inspect her face in the mirror. The muted color of her dress highlighted the lingering bruises under her eyes. Her shoulders started to sag once more.

The door clicked open, and Viviann jumped, surprised to see Evelyn back so quick. The maid's pulse was so intense, Viviann could see it throbbing at her neck. Evelyn held out an unsteady hand that contained a wrinkled, stained letter.

"It's not exactly a confession of suicide, but I found it in her bedside table after she died."

Viviann unfolded the letter, the paper crinkling in her fingertips, threatening to tear. It contained the thin, neat writing of her predecessor.

This house is a disease, a living monument to all the death this family has seen. I will not be a part of it.

ELEVEN

Viviann sat on her knees with all the ledgers and documents from the lawyer spread out beyond her, in chronological order. She wrote down from memory what the doctor had said and pieced together small bits of information she gathered from Peter's late-night chats and William's journal, which she also laid out, this time on the sofa since she was running out of floor space.

The list of mysterious happenings at the house was extensive, and it all started with William Halsby, builder of the house. It was clear to her, at this point, that he had strangled his wife and then killed himself in a state of madness, which would explain his last few journal entries.

Then there was the death of his female children, first Marie during childbirth, with some notes from her doctor that said she was exhibiting signs of losing her mind throughout her pregnancy. Then Josephine, of a mysterious childhood sickness that left her permanently weak. Next, Charles -Peter's uncle- was taken to a sanitorium in 1799 (which, Viviann learned, had cost the Halsby family thousands of pounds). Of course, there was the servant girl, Viviann couldn't forget, who had fallen into a fireplace while she was lighting it and burned to death.

Then there was Erica Taffer, who died after she had fallen and caught her head on the corner of a guest room side table. Viviann added next to the document, *William Jr.'s mistress? Did he kill her?* It wasn't long after her death that William Jr. was taken to a sanitorium as well, where he died of old age.

A servant boy died of thirst while trapped in the vines outside the house in 1806, Harriet died of hysteria in 1821, and then Elizabeth's suicide just two years ago. There was so much death surrounding this house. Viviann combed through the remains of William's journal once more but found no epiphany. She had originally thought the answers to this family's mystery lay in his tome, but now she wondered if it was scattered on the floor in front of her.

It was a question Viviann couldn't stop asking herself as the days moved on, bringing her closer to the party that was to be held in her honor. The house was an explosion of activity; maids ran around day and night, cleaning everything they could. Curtains were taken down and washed, carpets were scrubbed, furniture was polished, and windows were being opened and cleaned constantly. Where the house had been grim and dirty, now stood a mansion in almost perfect order. Viviann wandered the rooms in a daze, reaching out to touch every detail; details that had gone completely unnoticed until now.

On the day of the ball, while the sun was still up, Viviann and Evelyn were in her dressing room. Evelyn clasped the last few buttons on the bodice and stepped back so Viviann could take a look. Her breath caught when she could see her full self in the mirror. Her hair was still down and her person devoid of any jewelry, but still she looked like a duchess. Fit for a hostess of the Halsby manor. The pink silk glowed in the last bit of sunlight and complimented her now flawless skin.

"You look beautiful, my lady," Evelyn beamed. She guided her mistress to the vanity so she could start on her hair.

When Evelyn finished pulling her hair into braids and piling them on top of her head, Viviann decided to check on the rest of the house, making sure everything was prepared for tonight. She stood up straighter than she ever had; the echo of her expensive heels followed her wherever she went. The tile floors of the entry gleamed in the cozy candlelight. The banister, polished just this morning, was equally as glossy. It was a magnificent house. Fit for a queen.

This must've been what it was like for William to walk these halls almost a century ago. To feel true pride in owning such greatness. Viviann found herself in the great room so she could sneak a look at his painting. The sensation of being watched was strong still, but she felt power in the knowledge she held. She studied the journal in the painting. Was it the same? She imagined there must have been others, especially since the floating page that fell out of the book didn't seem to fit any of the torn pages. Did William throw them in the fire as well? She looked into the painting's eyes, hoping for an answer.

Maybe it didn't matter. She wondered if she would have her own portrait someday and hoped it would be as powerful as William's. Viviann continued her walk through the house, and ended up in the conservatory, which was as warm as a summer day, even on such a cold November night. The long rows of green plants and bright flowers were a welcomed sight. Viviann ran a hand through the leaves as she passed, making her way towards the glass paneled door that led to the garden. Just as she reached for the handle, something inside her stopped her dead in her tracks. Her mind grew fuzzy, and she stumbled backward; barely catching herself before she fell. She gripped the sides of a nearby planter while the sharp ends of palm fronds stabbed at her face and shoulders.

What was she doing here? She looked down at herself and noticed her elegant gown. Why was she wearing this? She righted herself and took a deep breath. Perhaps some fresh air would help clear her head. She propelled herself towards the glass door before she could stop herself and stumbled through the threshold. A rush of cold wind blew through her, wiping the fuzziness away instantly. She didn't even bother closing the door behind her.

What was all that? Viviann clutched her stomach, worried that it was the baby. She felt fine now, only a tad dizzy, like the morning after a drink. She wandered further down the path, following the last bits of sun as it peered through the trees.

Before long, she found herself approaching the gate to the cemetery. She couldn't believe it had taken her this long to end up here. The rusted scrap of iron shrieked while she pushed her way through. The light was fading fast, but her curiosity was too strong. The patch of land was severely overgrown, and some headstones were overtaken by underbrush and tree roots. Her heels threatened to sink into the soft dirt, but she kept on. She was looking for someone.

She passed by graves with names she was quite familiar with: Josephine Halsby, who was labeled "Too fragile for this world;" Charles Halsby, who had nothing on his gravestone besides his name; and then Marie Halsby-Alcott. She had a statue rising from the dirt, a beautiful woman in flowing robes with a baby in her arms. Below her name was another, *Lily Halsby Alcott*, with the same death day as her mother. Viviann placed a hand over her stomach, hidden beneath layers of pink silk.

Something in the corner of her eye caught her attention. It was another statue, this time of an angel with arms outstretched. It was pristine like it had just been sculpted, unlike Marie's which was layered with moss and decay. Viviann inched closer, her gown like a diminishing candle, surrounded by the dark night.

William Halsby

It was in the middle of the cemetery, awkwardly placed to Viviann's eye. This must've been where William had buried himself, and the rest of his family had been buried around him. Who had found him? And how long did it take one to suffocate under the weight of so much dirt? The never-ending list of questions ran through Viviann's mind again and again. William himself thought the house was cursed. He built it with his own two hands, a castle fit for a king, and then what? Did he just turn mad? She wondered if *she* was mad, obsessed with a man who had been dead for over seventy years. But that feeling inside her persisted, the dread and nausea. It felt like she was emerging from a thick fog, but instead of clarity she found a dropping sensation that rivaled her worst nightmares.

Fit for a king. It was something written in William's diary. She remembered having a similar thought when she walked downstairs just moments ago. It was chilling, to think of her thoughts as something other than her own. Not even ten minutes before she was feeling grateful to have been married into such a family, to have this house to call home. What was wrong with her?

She looked up at the house.

It was so tall she had to crane her neck to see its entirety. The first-floor windows were bright in the fading light, but the larger windows on the top levels were ominously dark. Ivy covered almost every inch of free space the back of the house held. *Fit for a king.* A whole line of them. What a contrast to all the death that surrounded her. Countless victims of the same disease, being a Halsby. That's what Elizabeth meant in her note. The survivors were a very narrow list, with no room for overgrowth. And if there was, it was quickly snuffed out.

She could no longer stand it. Any of it. She dashed back to the house. As she approached the conservatory door, she saw the rows of dying plants crowding the aisles. Not a flower in sight. Her fear was edging into rage.

Viviann hurried past the threshold and stomped towards the rest of the house.

"Stay out of my head," she muttered. A fogginess developed in her vision, slowly, like she was going to pass out. "Stay out of my head!" She screamed to the empty room.

Viviann took the grand staircase two steps at a time when she came to it, yanking her skirts high to enable her to run. Servants, alarmed at her sudden entrance, were too stunned to question her, and she slipped upstairs in silence. The guests would start arriving any minute, but she didn't care. She was going to tell Peter everything she had learned; show him William's journal and Elizabeth's note. He would have to believe her. And then they could leave this sickening place.

She burst into her bedroom. She bent down to reach for the wrapped book under her bed, but her hands brushed empty air and carpet. Blood pumped in her ears. She got down on her hands and knees and pulled up the bed sheet. Nothing. Just a dark open space. Viviann tore through her side table, thinking she must've put it in one of the drawers. Still, nothing. She was breathing hard now, and her head was growing fuzzier by the minute. She had stashed it under the bed. She knew she did. She tore through the rest of the room next, even searching through Peter's nightstand. It was gone. Taking a deep inhale, she moved on to her morning room, where she kept Elizabeth's note in the back of the lowest drawer, crumpled into a tight ball. She pulled it out in a flourish, her pulse calming as she looked at Elizabeth's dainty scrawl. *I will have no part in it.*

On a whim, she tried looking for the journal in her desk. She checked hiding places she never had considered before. Absurd ones too, like the small barrel that kept the fire stokers. Nothing.

Exhausted, Viviann rested her elbow on the mantle, allowing herself a moment to breathe. It shifted a brick on the fireplace's wall, and slowly a seam developed in the light-colored wallpaper. Viviann watched in awe.

Another hidden room, just like in the library. The grip of temptation was too strong. There could be other journals; she had to check. She pulled the mantle slightly and the fireplace swung open like a door. Beyond the opening was a sea of black. She crept inside to take a closer look. The fireplace swung backward without a sound, sealing Viviann inside with a scream.

TWELVE

The fire in Peter's study barely lit the room enough for him to search his desk. He was looking for a box of cigars he knew he put somewhere, saved for an occasion such as this. He shifted through piles of books that littered every surface, and moved onto the shelves next, filled with family heirlooms and trinkets from his travels. The carpet was dark, just like everything else, hiding the many stains he knew were lurking on it. He never let maids clean in here, lest they break something or get into his files, but a boy came every morning to light a fire in the fireplace. He doubted the boy had seen his cigar box, though.

He didn't notice the small knock at the door, nor the growing sliver of light as the door opened.

"Forgive me, my lord," he heard behind him, making him jump.

It was Evelyn, wearing her usual black dress and sleek bun, but she was wringing her hands nervously.

"Mrs. Winslet. Is everything alright?"

"Actually, my lord, Lady Viviann is missing. She got dressed for the ball and went downstairs for some air, but no one has seen her since."

"Missing? Well, have you checked- "

"Yes, my lord. I've checked everywhere. She's not here," Evelyn's tone was desperate, as were her eyes, like big black holes. She was seconds away from becoming hysterical.

He pulled out his pocket watch. Guests were due any minute. Panic began to set in as he thought of her accident. His eyes matched Evelyn's.

"It's too late to cancel the night, but we need to find her. I'll stall the guests as they arrive but get everyone downstairs to help search." Peter led Evelyn from the room, his voice becoming louder as they moved through the halls. "I'll tell everyone she's not feeling well while you find her. Benson!"

Mr. Benson was turning the corner just as Peter shouted his name.

"Her ladyship is missing. I need you and two footmen to stay with me in the ballroom."

Evelyn didn't wait to be dismissed, instead she took off running to the servant's hall, calling anyone she could think of.

"My lord?" Benson asked. "What's going on?"

"I don't know, but we have a party to host." As he said this, he heard a carriage approach down the drive. Benson hurried to the prepared bar that was overflowing with champagne, rum, and any other drink a guest could possibly want. A pyramid of their finest glasses was on the other side, and a footman fussed with the tablecloth, smoothing it down for the third time since Peter walked in.

Benson cleared his throat and snapped his fingers at the boy. The boy jumped and scurried to the front door.

Peter smoothed down his own suit and took a deep breath. His heart slammed in his chest.

When all traces of the sun's light had disappeared behind the wild woods beyond the house, more carriages began to arrive. Men, wearing their best suits and coats, were guided out of their carriages by their attendees. Ladies, dripping in expensive jewelry and fine silk, stepped out next, letting their large hoop skirts flourish around them. Vibrant hues of blue and silver were the most popular, adorned with impressive ruffles or bows.

Each guest was dazzled by the grandeur of the house, as well as its cleanliness. Every surface seemed to sparkle and radiate life. Peter stood just beyond the threshold, welcoming guests inside with his warm smile, hiding the anxiety he felt in his core.

"And where is the Hostess?" asked Mrs. Alberta.

Peter shook hands with her husband, Philip, who was the estate's agent. "She's not feeling well, I'm afraid. Just before everyone showed up, too. I do hope you understand."

"If anyone understands, it's us," Philip chuckled. "We have five boys at home, you know." They walked on.

Peter's lie became easier with every guest he told. He almost began believing it, until John and Jane Clarke entered the house. His mouth went dry and his smile slack.

"Peter, my boy," John yelled, arms outstretched as they walked over. Jane's eyes were shining while she took in the house. Peter winced when she turned her eyes on him. He awkwardly shook John's hand and kissed Jane's.

"It's so good to see you again!" She exclaimed. "Where is Viviann?"

"Oh, she... uh, she just went upstairs you see," Peter stumbled through his words. "You just missed her. She's not feeling well and decided to lay down for a while."

"How unfortunate. I'll see to her myself upstairs," Jane said, turning to the stairs.

"No!" Peter said too loudly, drawing the attention of all the guests nearby. Jane's painted eyebrows were so high they could have touched her hair line. Even the music momentarily stopped.

"I'm sorry Mrs. Clarke, her ladyship asked that she be alone during this time," Peter recovered.

"Her ladyship…" Jane muttered under her breath, turning back to the party. The rest of the guests went back to their conversations. Peter swiped his brow while the Clarkes made their way to the drink's table. His rapid beating heart couldn't take much more of Viviann's absence.

Evelyn's bottom half was covered in mud by the time she caught site of the house again. Her lantern gave her just enough light to see directly in front of her, but her feet still kicked up dirt and underbrush, coating the bottom of her shoes and making them slick. A cold wind picked up while they were out there, and she was chilled to the bone. Flashes of finding Elizabeth, bleeding out in the bath, dashed in and out of Evelyn's mind. That was not going to happen, Evelyn repeated to herself.

"Still nothing?" Asked a footman she hadn't seen draw near.

Evelyn flinched and almost tripped. "Nothing. We'll check upstairs again."

Some maids had said they saw Viviann running through the halls just before the party started, but they already checked the house and were forced to move to the grounds. The Halsby's carriage still sat in the carriage house, their horses still in the stable. It was like she had disappeared into thin air.

The house felt stifling hot as she took the servant's staircase two at a time, still drenched in mud. There had to be a place she hadn't looked. Evelyn checked the bedroom again and found nothing. She checked the morning room next, taking time to look through Viviann's desk for clues, which she had blown through the first time. A great stack of ledgers and folders sat on top of the desk. One of the thicker binders fell with a CLUNK when Evelyn tried looking through the stack. As she reached down to retrieve it, she heard a thumping noise beyond the walls. Evelyn jumped. She thought it might be the music from downstairs, but it was off key from what the musicians were playing. Was the house playing tricks on her again?

The thumping started anew, with the faintest sound underneath it, dull and low, like a scream beneath a pillow. Evelyn stepped up to the fireplace and watched as some knick-knacks rattled on the mantle in rhythm to the thumping. She gingerly placed her ear to the wall, her breath caught in her throat.

Get me out of here!

It was like a whisper, like it was coming from the wall itself. *Please, let me out of here!*

It was Viviann! When Evelyn connected the dots, she scrambled to do something. There was nothing beyond the wall, there couldn't be. She touched every surface of the fireplace, even clearing out all the logs and searching through the ashes for some sort of key, or knob, or door. With her hands covered in soot, she ran her fingers over every edge, corner, and crevice the fireplace held.

She pushed the tiles along the walls until she found one that actually slid inward. A seal developed down the wallpaper. Evelyn pried it open and Viviann's screams filled the air. A flash of hair and hands and silk caught Evelyn in the face, and she tumbled to the floor with her mistress on top of her.

Viviann was crying and still screaming, and her hands were bloody from ripping at the stone walls she was confined in. Her hair was a mess about her face and her voice came out hoarse from so much screaming. She looked like an animal, and the sobs that gripped her were almost primal.

Evelyn was already ripping at the bottom of her own dress, her muscle memory taking over as she felt for Viviann's wrists. She had torn a chunk of fabric loose but found nothing marring Viviann's skin. No cuts. No blood. Evelyn finally took in the scene with the open fireplace beyond them.

"My lady, what happened?" She demanded, shaking the poor woman. A seed of dread grew in Evelyn's belly.

"It was the house!" Viviann screamed. Her cheeks were as pink as her dress. "I can't take any more of this. I can't raise a child here, I won't! I need to get out of here. I'm leaving. Tonight! Please pack my things as quickly as possible, I'll grab Peter and then we can leave."

She was raving mad. Evelyn tried to calm her down; explain that the party was downstairs, but she wouldn't hear it.

"Please, Evelyn, I can't do this. Just go pack my things so we can leave," Viviann pleaded. Evelyn's mouth was agape, but no sound escaped. Viviann ripped her arm away before Evelyn could stop her and ran from the room, her long blonde hair trailing in her wake.

"Peter!" Viviann screamed as she went, her voice giving out.

She rounded the corner of the grand staircase and there he was, standing at the top step, shocked. She finally understood Evelyn's words about the party as the guests came into view, gaping up at her like she was a rabid dog. She saw her mother in the crowd, frozen as well. Viviann was quite a sight to behold. The hemline of her dress was dirty and torn, she was barefoot, and her hair was a lion's mane around her, halo-like in the room's candlelight. The blood caked around her fingers was the most unsightly, like something out of a child's bedtime story.

"Viviann," Peter breathed. "Where have you- "

"Peter, we need to leave now. It's not safe here."

Evelyn was behind her, trying to grab her by the arm and lead her back to her room. "My lady, it's okay, just come with me. We'll sort this out."

"Don't touch me!" Viviann tore her arm from Evelyn's grasp again. "I'm leaving."

She evaded Peter's hold as well and hurried down the steps. The door was in sight. She was going to take a horse and ride it until she reached her parent's, her real home. She didn't care how long it took her or if she dropped dead on the journey.

A force like the wind, strong and cold, shoved Viviann from behind so hard she lost her breath and her footing. She fell down the steps with a series of deafening cracks, the sound of bones or floorboards. Women screamed at the sight and men leapt in to save her, but it was too late.

Viviann landed amid a cluster of guests, in a pile of limbs and crinoline, at the bottom of the staircase. She was alive; everyone could hear her muffled sobs. She twisted in pain. Peter and Evelyn leapt down the steps in horror. They could hardly make out her face as they bent down towards her.

"What are you just standing there for," he screamed, scattering their guests. "Doctor! Please, help her!"

Dr. Salinger stood in the corner with his young wife, his champagne glass quivering in his hands. He looked like he had seen a ghost.

Evelyn hovered a shaky hand over her mistress' small form. "Viviann? Can you hear me?"

"Damn you!" Peter roared as he rounded on the pale doctor. "Help her! For God's sake, she's with child!"

Viviann clutched her stomach like she was going to retch, trembling like she had a fever. Ladies held their hands over their mouths, and the gentlemen looked equally horrified. Even Viviann's parents didn't dare move. Blood soaked the bottom of Viviann's gown, and before Peter and Evelyn had a chance to pick her up and carry her to the bedroom, she had left a large and unsettling stain on the carpet, a reminder of what the house had done.

The creaking of the staircase as they carried her sounded unmistakably like laughter.

THIRTEEN

Viviann woke in her bed the next morning, her insides sore. The back of her throat was marred after all her screaming, and sharp pain overwhelmed her every time she tried to swallow.

She hadn't really slept, just slipped in and out of consciousness until it was too bright outside to ignore. She was wearing the third nightgown that Evelyn had dressed her in, changing the old one when it became too bloody. There were some faint pink spots on the one she currently wore, and it looked like the bleeding had stopped hours ago. The silence was heavy in the large room, compared to the deafening noise from last night when they carried her in. Her own screams rang in her ears, combined with the shouts of Peter and the doctor, and even the shrill voice of her mother as they fought over her "accident." Another *accident.*

"It would be a miracle if Lady Halsby is able to carry the child to term," Dr. Salinger whispered to Peter in the hallway. "I wouldn't get your hopes up."

Her mother, listening through the door, gasped into her hand, looking more forlorn than Viviann had ever seen her.

Her mother had spent the night in her room, as did Evelyn. They sat in matching chairs, one on each side of the bed. They both dozed in the plush seats, both in the same attire they wore the night before; her mother in her gaudy evening gown and Evelyn in her somber maid's uniform, still caked with mud.

Evelyn stirred shortly after Viviann. Upon seeing her awake, Evelyn placed a calloused hand on top of hers.

"How are you feeling, my lady?" Evelyn whispered.

"Numb."

It was true. Her burning stubbornness from last night had faded into apathy. The house knew her every move it seemed. There was no escaping its reach.

"Please leave us." It was her mother, her voice calm and sharp. Evelyn and Viviann both jumped. Jane's intense stare across the blankets matched the maid's. "I need to speak with my daughter. Alone."

Evelyn looked at Viviann, daring her to dismiss her. Viviann didn't return her gaze and nodded towards the door. Without a word, Evelyn got up and slipped out.

The awkward tension between mother and daughter was thick, but Viviann didn't have the energy to remedy it.

"You made a mockery out of yourself last night," Jane said through gritted teeth.

Viviann let out a hoarse laugh. "That's what you're worried about right now? What the strangers from last night think about us? Think about you?"

"Those were Halsbrook's elite, Viviann. People you'll be surrounded with your entire life. And they will never forget," Jane spat.

"You think I care?" Viviann tried to shout. Her voice gave out halfway, resulting in a grating whisper.

"I know you don't care. That's the problem."

Viviann was silent, biting back burning tears. Jane let out a sigh and softened. "Viviann, my dear, you have been through so much. Don't think me not sympathetic, because I am. You're my child. When you're hurt, I hurt. But there comes a time when one must handle these things with an element of grace. It's the nature of the position you have married into."

There was a throbbing pain in Viviann's heart as her mother said this, but it was hardening, like a puddle of water freezing from the surface down. She was transported back to a memory of a scene not unlike the one unfolding in front of her. It was a miserable morning, just after dawn, when she heard a carriage pull up to Edward's house.

Viviann was laying in Edward's empty bed. The undertaker had left an hour ago. Jane opened the door with a gasp. Edward's mother stood behind her, arms crossed. Her eyes were red, but they were dry.

"Viviann..." her mother started, unable to finish.

"I just wanted to be close to him before he..." Viviann choked. The tears bubbled up again and were soon bursting from her tired eyes. Her body rocked with her violent sobs.

"She was like this when they came for him." Edward's mother spat out the words.

"Viviann, it's time to go."

Viviann only sobbed harder, twisting the sheets in her hands. It took two young footmen from Edward's household to rip her out of his bed. She could hear her mother's apologizes and condolences in between her own ferocious screams. There was the slam of the front door just after they crossed the threshold and the slam of the carriage door after the footmen had loaded her in. Viviann was alone in the freezing carriage for what felt like an hour, until she was completely chilled to the bone. She was wearing only her slip and a cloak her mother had brought for her. Her dress still lay on the floor next to Edward's bed. The cold slowly calmed her down. She no longer thought of feeling Edward's breath against her chest while she held him last night, or the terror she experienced upon waking up and realizing he was already gone.

Her mother shoved herself into the carriage and soon the horses were pulling them away. "I swear to God, Viviann, if I ever see that kind of behavior again, I will disown you as a daughter. How embarrassing for us. I know you're upset and trust me- your father and I are as upset as well-, but you need to have a handle on your emotions. Especially in the presence of others."

Viviann only half heard this. Her head was pressed against the carriage's window, her cheek frozen where it made contact with the glass. All she could think about was the coldness spreading over her. The numbness went all the way to her heart, clawing through her skin as it spread.

She felt a similar numbness as she laid in the Halsby manor, under the down quilt. The same disdain covered Jane's face as she stared at her from across the bed.

"I think Viviann needs her rest," a strong voice said from the darkness of the doorway. Peter stepped out of the shadows. "And I think you need to leave, Mrs. Clarke."

Jane stood up abruptly, shocked by his directness. Dark shadows fell beneath his eyes like he hadn't slept through the night either. Evelyn emerged from the shadows next, arms crossed, and her form almost completed hidden by Peter's figure. Jane left with a curt nod and a swish of her ballgown. Viviann felt something swell in her chest as she looked up at her husband, and although it was buried deep, under all the fear and exhaustion, she knew it was love.

FOURTEEN

The party that had quickly become a disaster became infamous among the inhabitants of Halsbrook. Poor Viviann was out of her mind, they said. Just like that Elizabeth. Although most of the guests from that night could've sworn Viviann had been pushed by an unknown force, they began convincing themselves Viviann must've tripped on her hemline.

Viviann didn't care what the town said about her, though. She didn't care about much of anything anymore. Days quickly bled into weeks.

Night after night, Viviann suffered terrible nightmares. She would find herself in one of the corridors in the house, but every time she tried to walk into a room, the door would disappear, and darkness would fall heavy over her shoulders. Sometimes, something would be chasing her through the blackness. Other times, she found herself dangling off a cliff or balcony, until her fingertips could no longer hold her, and she would fall to her death. Her whole body would be coated with sweat like she had a fever, and her nightgown would be slick against her skin. Her screams would eventually turn into sobs, and Peter could hold her for a moment while she thrashed about, trying to coax her awake. Sometimes nothing would be able to wake her, and Peter would have to run down the servant staircase in his robe and bare feet, calling for Evelyn.

After one of her weekly doctor visits, Peter stopped Dr. Salinger in the hall just outside their bedroom. "Doctor, please understand this does not come from a place of disrespect, but... she's not getting any better."

"Better?" Dr. Salinger twisted around and peaked through the crack of the door. Viviann was already asleep.

"Yes, she's still so agitated and...different. She's so different now. It's like she's hollow."

Dr. Salinger sighed and clasped the other man's shoulder. "Lord Halsby, your wife has undergone a great deal of stress. I'm not sure she'll ever be the same."

"So there's nothing you can do? There's nothing you can give her?"

"Even if there was something, who knows how the child might react to it. I'm sorry." The doctor tipped his hat and left.

Peter watched him go, waited for him to round the corner before he turned and slammed his fist into the wall, through the wallpaper and plaster. The sound rippled through the silent house, and the midwife that was still in their room let out a frightened scream and dropped the pitcher of water she was holding. The shatter was almost as loud as his fist's blow. He heard Viviann stir from beyond the door. He rubbed his jaw with his hands, feeling the stubble across his chin. Footsteps came toward him fast from the other side of the house and he knew it would be Evelyn. The maid was never too far from Viviann's side at all times. He slipped downstairs to his study without being seen and locked the door behind him.

In an attempt to cheer her up some weeks later, Peter called a local artist to the house. Evelyn pulled out one of Viviann's Arrosborough gowns, one of the oldest she had, forest green with a dramatic collar. Even though it couldn't have been more than four years old, it looked unfashionable compared to the other gowns in the wardrobe. The surprise she showed when she first saw the dress was the most emotion she had displayed in two months since her bed rest had started.

"I thought it would be quite nice to have a bit of home in your portrait," Evelyn said as she dressed her, moving around her like she was made of glass. She still wore no corset, so it looked different than it did when Viviann had it made. It was tighter in the waist and looser in the arms than it should have been, but Viviann didn't care enough to fight Evelyn on it. She didn't care about anything anymore.

She didn't care to be friendly with the artist when she met him and sat in the high back chair he had chosen without worrying about what her hair looked like or how her dress had settled. The artist himself was a small shy man, drowning in clothes much too big for him, sitting behind a massive canvas.

"Your ladyship, will you move your chin slightly to the left? Thank you." His voice was as soft as a whisper. They were seated in her morning room, her first time in it since the party. It felt odd to be there with a stranger, usually guests were entertained downstairs in the drawing room, but Viviann was told not to attempt the stairs until the baby was born. It was just as well, her meals were brought to her room and Peter spent much of his time after dinner in her bedroom, sitting by the fireplace, reading.

Viviann focused on the afternoon light fading in through the leaded glass, wondering what her portrait would look like. Would it have the same eerie quality as the rest? Peter had said this was a new artist to the family, and her portrait would be one of a kind for a while, at least until they decided when their child's portrait would be done. Viviann stopped listening after he said this. Her mind stayed far away from the thing in her stomach, if she could help it.

After a long three hours, when the base of her spine started to numb, the artist expressed his gratitude for her patience and dismissed her. She came over to his workstation, meticulously organized and clean, to see how she looked so far. It was a rough sketch of her and her environment with a few tests of color that he would use as reference as he finished the painting over the next month or so. Viviann let out a small laugh when she saw herself. The artist was mortified at her response, almost knocking over his tin of white paint.

"I'm so sorry," she quickly recovered, trying not to smile. "It looks like it's going to be wonderful. I'm relieved, actually. I thought it was going to..." she trailed off.

The artist seemed satisfied and packed up the remainder of his things. He would pick up the painting the following morning when it had dried, and once he was gone for the evening, Viviann snuck back into the morning room for another look. It really did look like it would turn out wonderful, with his color swatches matching her the colors of her gown exactly. She looked so ordinary, in the best of ways. It looked like a painting that could be found in every house across England. There was nothing strange or unsettling about it. No eyes that seemed to follow you down the hall. It was like peering through a looking glass. She knew she would look exhausted, with the dark half-moons under her eyes and her sunken in cheeks, but she was surprised that she didn't look as defeated as she felt. Perhaps that was the artist's generosity, like painting a straight nose when it was in fact crooked. She held her head high in the painting, with her shoulders back, like she had conquered quite a beast.

Was it possible, then, for her to feel something besides the hollowness that pervaded under her skin? She placed a hand over her stomach, wondering if she wasn't hollow after all. For the first time since falling pregnant, Viviann found herself hoping whatever it was inside her still lived.

That night, Viviann woke to a searing pain in her stomach. She bolted upright and felt a wave of fear take hold of her heart. Was this the moment the doctor had been waiting for? For the baby to finally give up after so much trauma? It was still dark, and the room around her was covered in shadows. In a flash the pain was gone. Peter stirred.

"What's going on? Are you alright?"

"I'm not sure. I woke up to this pain-" Viviann's words were choked off with a deep groan.

Viviann could feel the cramps throughout her body, but strongest in her stomach and lower back. Like a wave, it came and went, but a severe pressure in her abdomen was constant. Viviann finally felt how wet the sheets were underneath her.

"The baby's coming," she could hardly say.

Like a man on fire, Peter leapt from the bed and out of the room, screaming for the midwife and any servant he could name. There was a level of terror in his voice that forced everyone from their beds to the first floor. When news of the impending arrival spread through the servants, the house was alive with commotion. A boy was sent on a horse to retrieve the doctor, while Evelyn held Viviann's hand through the contractions. The midwife coached her through the pain, and maids helped change her sheets and clothes, as well as prepared all the hot water they would need.

The morning sun was bleeding through the curtains before Viviann began to push. Her screams could be heard as far as the carriage house. Peter roamed the halls restlessly, smoking a pipe and running his hands through his unmade hair, still in his night robe.

The rest of the servants carried on with their duties with knowing looks and somber faces. Not one person dared to tempt fate by talking about the unborn child.

Finally, in the bright light of the afternoon, the cries of a baby could be heard from the bedroom. It was such a soft sound, compared to Viviann's howling that had lasted for most of the day. The midwife opened the door, revealing Dr. Salinger wiping his hands on a cloth, Evelyn standing over Viviann, her face wet with tears, and Viviann pale and exhausted, holding the crying baby in her limp arms. Peter rushed over.

"Congratulations, your lordship. It's a baby girl."

She was a small little thing; her head was no bigger than Viviann's hand. Her cries were becoming deeper and more powerful with every passing minute. Healthy. Through sunken eyes, Viviann stared down at her daughter. The baby's eyelashes were long already, and small wisps of light hair collected on top of her head. Viviann held the baby against her chest, with her heart beating fast and her body exhausted. Peter bent over her and kissed the top of her head, his own eyes bleary. He softly caressed the baby's cheek, so pink and soft.

"A name, your ladyship," asked the midwife. "What will the name be?"

"Julia," Viviann breathed. "Julia Halsby." She looked up at Peter and they kissed, long and slow, for one of the first times since their wedding.

FIFTEEN

After Julia was born, Viviann's every waking hour was spent doting on her. Her nightmares seemed to cease, but that was simply due to her lack of sleep. At the end of the day, Viviann would be so mentally and physically fatigued she would collapse into bed; thrust headlong into a dreamless sleep.

"Viviann, please. You're exhausted. It can't be good for the baby," Peter pleaded.

"I think I'll decide what's good for my baby," Viviann retorted, placing Julia against her breast to suckle.

Peter had hired yet another wet nurse and had the audacity to bring her upstairs. Viviann glared at the woman, who already looked terrified of her. She was aware of the whispers around town.

"Now, get out."

Viviann and Peter's bedroom soon became just Viviann's room, even after the nursery was completed. Since no one suspected the child to survive, the nursery was only thought about after her arrival. One of the smaller guest rooms on the second floor was quickly converted. The servants dug out the Halsby crib from the attic that had been used for generations. With a thorough dusting and a coating of polish, it looked as good as new. Viviann asked for a chair to be brought up so she could sit with the baby, and many nights passed as she slept in the chair. Any amount of noise would startle Viviann awake, and she would peek into Julia's crib where she would always be sleeping soundly.

Julia was beautiful, even when she cried, which was often. She had deep blue eyes, the color of a stormy sea, with speckles of brown and gold toward the edges. Viviann was delighted to find Julia looked like her, even if it was slight. The white wisps of hair that soon grew into a full set of short curls was the most striking resemblance between them.

It took Viviann a year to sit with Peter at dinner, instead of taking it in her room. Peter was aghast when he saw Viviann's form slip through the dining room door. She sat down without looking at him and took a serving of roast duck that a footman bent down to offer to her. Benson, holding a decanter of dark wine, exchanged glances with Peter. Three more courses followed in silence, but it was something.

This, of course, was due to Evelyn's persistence. Every day, Viviann dabbled more and more into the habits of her former self and became a lady once again. Evelyn would ask her question after question that she could have easily answered herself, but it forced Viviann to have an opinion again, and be active in her role as mistress of the house. Viviann noticed how everyone treated her differently when she started performing simple tasks like sending out letters (all to her mother) or asking for a cup of tea to be brought up to her morning room while she completed some embroidery. It was like they wanted to congratulate her on being alive. Most of the time it made her feel worse, in the pit of her heart where she thought she had long buried her emotions, but it was nice too.

Being alive *was* difficult, and she felt like she did deserve a pat on the back for making it this far. The servants no longer snuck away from her if they heard her approaching in the hall, and they started looking to her again for decisions instead of leaving it to Mrs. Avery and Benson. They also started including her in the gossip of the household. One of the younger housemaids, Louise, had a terrible crush on the delivery boy that carried fresh food in from the village every week. Anne, another housemaid, was in mourning for her sister, who died from a fever that seemed to be going around. Viviann avoided the girl at all costs; when she saw the maid's black band around her sleeve, all she could see was the poor girl's sister, laying in a pool of sweat. This thought stirred up memories of Edward, dusty ones, like a loose sketch buried deep in a drawer in her mind.

Viviann liked her routine, and it kept the nightmares at bay. Julia was growing fast, and before Viviann knew it, she took her first steps in the drawing room. The girl was fascinated by new things and delighted in exploring new rooms. Her wobbly steps soon developed into sloppy running, but she was fast, and it sometimes took both Viviann and Robert, the footman, to catch her.

A nanny was hired, and not long after, the people in the village began to wonder about the miracle child that lived beyond the walls of the Halsby manor. Viviann was called to the homes of some of Halsbrook's wealthy families, despite the horrifying events of the party almost two years before. She asked them to come to the estate instead, which was what they really desired anyway. They wanted to see Poor Viviann in her natural habitat, where they had the ability to sneak away if she had another "episode."

"Julia is such a…free spirited child," Mrs. Wadsworth settled on during one of their luncheons in the garden. It was a gorgeous Spring day, making the Halsby House look even more like a dream.

Her and Viviann were watching Julia run like a mad woman through the delicate flowers just off the garden path. Her nanny followed close behind, shaking with nerves, calling out to her to slow down or to come back.

Viviann smiled at the condescending comment. Julia's joyful screams filled the air. For the first time since Viviann's fall, she felt happiness' shadow inside her. She had a beautiful, healthy child and she, herself, was in good health and relatively high spirits. There had been an unshakable feeling of emptiness that persisted inside

Viviann the last two years. But with the sun on her face, Julia's laugh ringing in her ears and the house behind her, she could have fooled herself that it was gone.

Later that evening, after Mrs. Wadsworth left and dinner had been served and eaten, Viviann found herself in the great room, sitting beneath William's gaze. Peter rubbed at his temples for the fourth time, letting out a painful hiss.

"Oh, for God's sake, Peter, tell me what's wrong."

"I don't feel like myself. It's just a headache, I'm sure. I don't want you worrying about me."

But she did; she was amazed that she did. What if during all the fuss over her and Julia, Peter's health had been forgotten and he could be rotting away from some brain fever. Her heart quickened at the thought of illness, no matter what kind, seeing Edward yet again on his death bed through her mind's eye. But Peter looked fine. He had been short with her at dinner, but that was it.

"Why don't we go upstairs and get some sleep," Viviann said, careful not to imply that they would sleep together.

"No, no it's fine. I'm alright. I just need a drink."

Viviann moved to the hidden bar. Doing something was better than just sitting. She tried not to think about the painting staring at her back. She filled a glass and decided last minute to fill another. She brought one to Peter, who had his head between his knees now, and placed it on the tea table in front of him. Viviann raised her own glass to her lips and tipped her head towards William. *Cheers*, she thought.

"Thank you for this," Peter said in a half whisper.

"Of course."

"No, I mean about spending time with me here."

Viviann felt a stab in her heart. She had only come here with him a handful of times since Julia was born, it was true, but she didn't want to think about how Peter had taken it.

"Of course," Viviann said again, slow and controlled. She took another sip of her drink, let the sherry burn down her throat and into her belly. "It was never about you, Peter."

Thunder cracked somewhere in the distance, and the light patter of rain could be heard just beyond the windowpanes.

"Was it not? That's how it seemed to me." There was no malice in his voice, just exhaustion and pain.

Viviann swallowed the rest of the sherry. "It was hard once Julia was born to be away from her, even for dinner or a drink."

"She could've joined us in here. We could turn this into a family room, spend some real quality time together."

There wasn't a chance in hell Viviann would let Julia in this room. She had the servants lock it in the afternoons so the child couldn't wander in behind Nanny's back.

"I feel like I never see her," Peter said from the rim of his glass. "I feel like I never see you."

"What do you mean? We have dinner together every night." Viviann knew her argument was weak, as their dinners were often short and without much conversation.

"We eat at the same table, but we don't spend time together. I feel like I don't know who you are anymore." He looked up at her from his seat with big, beseeching eyes.

Viviann sighed and sat down on the sofa across from him. Did he know who she was before this, before the house and Julia and the fear had taken everything from inside her? They had always been strangers. His words still hurt in an odd way, like she had failed some hidden test. But there was something else too, a tenderness. She didn't think he would care if she was here one way or another. The crackling fire next to them was the only sound in the room. The rain had stopped.

"I want to know you," Peter whispered. He rose from the chair and sat next to her. The sofa sagged under his weight and pushed her farther into him. She could smell the sherry and his cologne, a mix of sweet and sour. "Just give us a chance, Viviann."

Her cold heart melted at the sound of her name whispered so softly. She felt the onslaught of tears but held them back by nodding her head a few times. She had been alone for too long, and her desire for him inflamed. She responded with a kiss. A long, slow kiss filled with the hope that had collected in her over the years. He returned the kiss with a ferocious gusto.

He leaned her back towards the sofa's arm while she tried to peel off his suit jacket. She wanted to be as close to him as possible; she wanted to be in his skin. Taking off her dress would be a nightmare so they both violently pulled at her skirts.

Peter ran his lips down Viviann's neck, almost completely on top of her now, and whispered, "Let's make an heir."

Pleasure's hold on her released like a tight rope being cut. He was still trying to kiss her, still trying to unbutton his trousers, all with the look of a wild man. Viviann pushed him off her with all her might, kicking him in the stomach in the process. Peter crashed into the tea table, sending their teacups over the edge and onto the carpet.

"What's the matter with you?" Peter said, rubbing his rib.

Viviann opened her mouth a few times but couldn't make a sound. Instead, she buttoned her gown's collar with shaky hands. Peter sat still on the floor, breathing hard.

"Viviann, please, just tell me what's going on."

"I don't want any more children, Peter," Viviann blurted. There was a finality in her tone that surprised them both. William watched over them with sad eyes.

"What do you mean you don't want any more children? What about an heir?"

"Why can't Julia be the heir?"

"You know why. She's a woman. Someday she will marry someone, and this place will go to him and his name. Her children won't be Halsby's; she'll be the last one." Peter's voice shook with both fear and fury.

"I don't want any more children. End of discussion." Viviann rose from the sofa and smoothed her wrinkled skirts. She kept her head down, not willing to meet her husband's eyes nor William's. Peter snatched her wrist before she could walk away.

"End of discussion? You mustn't be serious, Viviann. You will not decide the fate of my family," he spat.

"This is my family now, too," Viviann retorted, though she didn't believe it. Julia was hers. It was the only part of this family she would ever have, and she intended to keep it that way.

"You certainly don't act like it," Peter said, using her wrist to haul himself up. "You act like coming here was a prison sentence."

"Let go of me."

"You don't understand the position I'm in," he raged. "I have a duty to my family, to this house, to continue the Halsby name." Peter's pupils were so dilated in the dim light she could hardly see his irises. She tried pulling her wrist away from him; his grip tightened.

"You're not going to stand in the way of that." It was then that Viviann realized how tall he was. Almost a foot taller than her. She looked up at his dark face. Viviann slapped him as hard as she could with her free hand. The hit echoed through the room as Peter stumbled away.

Viviann didn't wait for him to steady himself. She ran out in a blur of olive silk, crashing into one of the footmen as she dashed through the hallway. Distantly, she heard Benson calling her name, and the other footmen asking her if she was alright. The pulsing in her ears was too loud to distinguish what they were saying. She ran through them. She didn't stop until she was up the stairs and slamming her bedroom door, locking it behind her as she slid down the ornate wood, pulling her legs close to her for support. Tears ran down her face without her realizing she was crying.

SIXTEEN

The attic of the Halsby house was filled to the brim with clutter. Furniture, with sheets covering their surfaces, loomed like ghosts throughout the mess. The smell of dust and mildew immediately assaulted the senses and coated everything in sight, giving the room a hazy quality, like it was covered in smoke. Windows lined the back walls, small ones that peered out onto the outside roof, but they were covered in filth and more clutter, so it was as if there was no light at all.

Viviann stood at the front of the room with a single lantern, directing maids to her and Julia's fall and winter wardrobe, which were packed away into sturdy trunks at the start of the warm season.

Summer was ending any day now, but it was impossible to tell from the heat that saturated the attic. Viviann wiped sweat from her brow.

The group of maids in front of her extracted a trunk from a pile of debris. Just as they pulled it clear, one of the maids tripped over a wayward box and toppled some nearby crates with a deafening crash. Another maid shrieked as dust plumed around them, sending them each into coughing fits. With her eyes and lungs burning, Viviann reached for the fallen maid. The girl had started working for them only a week prior. She looked shaken, too afraid to accept her mistress' hand.

"I'm so sorry, Madame, I'm not usually this clumsy," the maid stammered through suppressed coughs.

"It's okay," Viviann assured. "Are you alright?"

The girl looked down at her dirty uniform and trembling hands. "I...I think so."

Well, she won't last long in this house, Viviann thought. She turned to the other maids. Their eyes darted from one side of the room to the other, some fidgeted with the ties of their aprons. The darkness in the attic was heavy around them, like a firm hand on everyone's shoulder. Viviann felt it too. She was extra jumpy since her and Peter's fight a week prior. She had kept the reins on her emotions so far, but the oppressive heat and darkness threatened her hold. Sweat soaked the back of her day dress.

"Let's move along ladies," Viviann said. The maids dragged the trunk the rest of the way and soon were carrying it down the stairs to her dressing room.

Viviann lingered behind. She couldn't care less about all the junk surrounding her, but the more she stared the more she found. Odd-shaped trinkets scattered the lantern-lit area in front of her, mingling with books so dusty their covers looked like they were made out of fur. She should go back; she knew she should, but her feet carried her forward and soon she hoisted her skirts to navigate the small foot space between forgotten items.

She passed children's toys, ladies' hat boxes, and chests of every size. An empty bird cage laid open on its side, almost swallowed by dust and decay. Against the toppled crates leaned a forgotten painting. She bent down and ran a hand across the surface, exposing the portraiture underneath. It was a woman, with dark hair pulled into an elaborate display on the top of her head. What was strange was that the woman wasn't looking at the painter. Instead, she was half turned, like she had heard something and looked away for a moment. Her mouth was slightly open, like she was about to say something. Viviann felt like the woman was right in front of her, her pose and facial expression so life like she almost expected her to turn back to the center of the canvas. The woman's dress was ornamented with a navy crinoline that was stretched neatly over her slim form, and the billowy sleeves caught the imaginary light like it was silk.

The realization struck Viviann like a slap. It was Elizabeth. She could feel it in her bones. After all this time, all her wondering, now she was here in front of her. Elizabeth was more beautiful than she imagined; Viviann found herself disappointed in the fact. She looked smaller and younger in this painting, even though she knew Elizabeth had been twenty when she married Peter. The same age Viviann was when she said "I do" two years later. Why would the artist paint her in this position? What was she looking at? It gave Viviann chills to think of an answer. She turned the portrait around so she wouldn't have to see it anymore. Dust lingered on her fingertips and then on her dress as she tried to rub it away.

She came to the fallen crates, their contents strewn across the attic floor. Something caught her eye; a sparkle as it reflected the light of her lantern. Nothing up here had a shine to it anymore. Whatever it was must've been well hidden in the ancient crate. She bent down to inspect the damage and saw a palm sized wooden box, laying in two pieces on the dust covered floor. The design on it was rudimentary in style, giving it the look of a new wood carver, an artisan not yet having mastered the craft. Not too far from the wreckage was a ring. It was heavier than she expected, especially for its size. The only ornamentation was a row of diamonds covering the band on one side. She picked up the broken box as well and placed the ring in the velvet interior. Her mind ran with the possibilities. Which Halsby's was it? She inspected her own wedding ring, simple in design as well, with a singular tear drop jewel the color of red wine. Or blood.

She inspected the rest of the crate's old contents, disturbing more clusters of dust. Within the remnants lay a medium sized journal, completely plain and tied with a strip of extra leather. It looked like a cleaner copy of William's journal. It couldn't be. Viviann snatched it before she could even think about it. She swiped her hand across the cover; it was layered with dust, but this time there was no ash. She slowly untied the journal and opened it to the first page.

William L. Halsby, 1750

A small loose paper slipped from between some pages, but Viviann managed to catch it before it floated to the ground. It was crisp from decades of sitting inside the journal, but it was almost translucent with age. She flipped it around.

London, 1749

We regret to inform you that your father, Christopher Halsby, and brother, Christian Halsby, have been killed during a mutiny while on route to India in the month of May, 1748.

The perpetrators of said mutiny have been dealt with. The East India Company thanks your family for their forty years of service.

January 8th, 1750

A week into the new year and already so much has changed. When I wrote last, I was still just William. A simple businessman. A father, a husband.

It's strange, knowing they're dead. It's strange because I don't really feel anything at all.

But now they're gone, and I am to inherit everything. I know little of what that means except there is an unfinished house in the countryside of northern England. I could stay as I am, remain in Paris, and let the state collect my father's fortune. But I can't deny the temptation I feel to give my children an English upbringing.

I suspect my father is rolling in his watery grave at the prospect of his second and worthless son being known as Lord Halsby. That morbid thought gives me more comfort than it should.

January 12th, 1750

Marguerite and I have decided to move to my father's estate. The children are most excited, since all they know about the country are the adventure stories I told them from when I was a boy. I think it will be good for them to grow up in the countryside rather than the city. Marguerite is apprehensive at best about the change, as she's never left France before. But I never loved Paris. I loved school, and when school was done, I loved Marguerite.

I know it is the nostalgia for my youth, brought on by the children's never-ending questions, that has me almost equally as excited. Not that it will be like my time growing up in Evermore, but one can hope.

I remember the green of the dancing grasses just outside the house. I remember the frogs me and Christian used to catch, before he had found pleasure in being cruel.

It's a memory I haven't thought about for many years. I think a part of me has repressed everything about the past, as I am unable to untangle the good from the horrible.

February 25th, 1750

Tomorrow we sail for England. My days have been filled with nothing but preparation for this journey, and yet I still feel as if I am missing something.

- *Check luggage*
- *Organize carriage to ship*
- *Find Zeus*

I'm not sure if Zeus is missing but I'd rather not risk Marie's happiness, since I know how much the girl loves that stuffed rabbit.

Everything seems to be in order. Then why do I still feel so ill at ease? Marguerite thinks it is because I will be surrounded once again by my father. She might be right. It's been fifteen years since I've seen him. He might be gone, but the house was built in his image and his possessions, I assume, reside at the estate.

It's not something I look forward to, rummaging through my father's things. I don't care to know the horrible things he's been up to since I left. Of course, he had been involved in the East Indian

Company since I was just a boy. When I wanted to go to college in Paris, it was made possible with the money he made through the company. Everything I am right now, is due to them. I have a comfortable life here. But I've heard the stories about what they do. My father's own men turned against him.

I don't think I care to know much more. They're gone anyway, so I guess it really doesn't matter now. What will I find when we land? How far along will the house be? Am I making the right choice by going back?

I worry I may never sleep if these thoughts keep up.

March 3rd, 1750

I feel as if the last week has shaved ten years off my life. It took us more than half a day to reach England. And what have we found? A skeleton of a house not fit to live in just yet.

We have taken up residence in the village inn. It is quite cramped with the five of us, but I guess we'll make do. The children and Marguerite are still overcoming their seasickness, so I imagine I will not see them out of bed for some time.

I've only seen the house once so far. The carriage driver nearly laughed at us when we asked him to take us, saying it was more of a "death trap" than a house. He was right. There were building materials and tools everywhere, but most of it is completely unrecognizable.

It took me half a day to even find bloody answers about the house. Where were all the workers? When would the work be finished?

I feel exhausted down to my bones. This is a nightmare. I'm trying to remain calm but how can I? I uprooted my whole family, and for what? So we could crowd in an inn?

March 14th, 1750

After almost a week, I finally met the workmen for my father's estate. I was feeling so anxious to start, so we could have a proper place to live, but now I just feel dread.

With the news of my father's death, the workers were sent back to the port where my father's ship had brought them, almost a day's journey away from here. I'm not surprised they didn't think anyone would be coming. Knowing my father, he probably told them I had died as a small boy, if he had even mentioned me at all.

When they arrived at the site, I think I was as surprised to see them as they were to see me. They all had incredibly dark skin and impossibly black hair. It didn't seem like they spoke one lick of English, or French for that matter. But the foreman spoke some English, thankfully, and he was able to tell me that some were taken from the coast of Africa, and the other from India. Taken.

It explained the three Englishmen that just stood around and watched them work. One of them said they were the "handlers." Disgusting men, those Englishmen are. One of them even had a whip on their hip. I've never seen anything like it. Deep down it makes me sick. I'm not sure why.

March 28th, 1750

I write from an inn at Port Else, where my father's things are being kept. I have seen the storehouse and the ships my father owned. I went through various treasures and pieces of furniture for hours today, wondering how my father had acquired all these things. Now they are mine. I want to light a match to it. It's better than what I really want to do, which is wrap my arms around the entirety of it and mourn the loss of my family.

They were cruel, to everyone. They did unspeakable things both to me and the people I love. Yet, I almost miss them. I fear I'm actually impressed by the things my father and Christian built together. The port speaks of them like they were fearsome gods. What would people say about me when I passed? Marguerite will say I was a kind husband, and hopefully the children will say I was a good father. Everyone else will be silent. Because there's nothing to say! I haven't built anything. I have no legacy for my children.

But now I do.

April 14th, 1750

I just want to sleep. I lay in bed for hours, changing to every position I can think of, counting the tiles in the ceiling, arranging my pillows in a number of ways. Still, I find no peace. I hear cries from somewhere beyond the inn, in the wilderness perhaps, or at the estate.

Half a dozen times I have brought myself up to the half-built house and wandered the empty rooms. Large stretches of canvas still line the newly laid hardwoods, and the smell of the fresh wallpaper practically chokes me. I check every window, every wall that's been erected so far, looking for any sort of mishap I feel certain is there. Nothing.

I feel faint with sleepiness during the day but when I lay down, I feel as restless as a caged animal. I walk for hours, hoping it will tire me out, and it does, I feel the tiredness down to my bones. I even fell in the forest while out walking yesterday.

One minute I was hurrying down the path in the village that leads towards the house, and the next I was laying on my back, miles within the forest, with a large and unsightly gash across my forehead. I must have fallen into some kind of trance and tripped over some underbrush or what have you.

The sight of me gave Marguerite quite a scare when I found my way back to our room. She put me on bedrest thinking my body must now like to sleep after suffering such an injury, but apparently not.

Now, I sit at the small desk the inn provides, hoping to feel some sense of ease at writing this down. I feel as if I am going mad. I just want to sleep. My wound aches greater now than it has since I woke up with it, and has made it hard to keep my focus on this page.

April 19th, 1750

A dream. Finally, after so long without sleeping, I was able to rest my head down, and drift away.

Last night I was visited by a messenger. A guide with icy hands and freezing breath. I was led to the clearing, where a dusting of snow covered the unfinished foundation of the manor. This skeleton of a future haven provided no protection against the biting winds.

As I walked through the unfinished doorframe I saw them, the pale-blue husk of my wife. Her arms curled like a dead spider's around the small boy in her arms. My son. My beautiful son. Eyes once full of life now glassy windows into an empty vessel, robbed of vitality by the bitter cold.

It's a premonition, I know it. I can still feel the cold, I can still see my dead family. The house must be completed.

May 16th, 1750

As of a week ago, I've started working on the house myself. My whole body aches, but it feels good to actually see progress. I've cut wood planks, hammered them in place. I spent all of yesterday laying carpet and wallpaper on every wall and floor in that house. Marguerite is going to love it; I can't wait to show it to her.

I'm slowly convincing her to allow the children to spend time here while we work. She's nervous about all the workers and how dangerous building can be, but they couldn't be safer. James is too young to start helping, but Jonathon is already fourteen -it's time for him to work hard and put some muscle on his bones. He'll be right by my side, helping me build the house that will one day be his.

For the first time since we've come here, I've actually felt hopeful. This could really be a home. A wonderful place to raise our family and watch our children have children and create a real legacy.

September 1st, 1750

I awoke last night covered in sweat. I suffered through another dream last night. It was more or less the same as the previous dreams I've described, except this time I found my entire family, not just Marguerite or one of the kids, but all of them. I could feel them. I could feel all of it. They were so cold. My fingers still ache from the snow, although it's been several hours since I woke.

I think I'm losing my mind. Or if I haven't already, then I will. What more can I do? The house is still not finished. It's the middle of August and hotter than the devil himself, but winter will be upon us before we know it. The men are slacking again. We were making unbelievable progress, but now, you'd guess they've never done a day of hard work in their life.

What am I going to do?

September 19th, 1750

The strangest thing happened a few nights ago, and I'm still trying to puzzle it out. I woke in the middle of the night to the sound of hammering. At first, I thought I was dreaming, but when I wandered toward the sound, I realized it was coming from the upstairs.

Ten men were on the third floor, finishing the walls that will later divide rooms. All the others were outside in the dirt, cutting wood and hammering metal into shape. It was the middle of the night. The workers should've gone back to their cots in the carriage house hours ago.

The truly strange part came when I tried asking them what they were still doing here. They acted like they couldn't hear me. They just continued what they were doing. When I got a closer look at all of them, they looked terrible, almost sick like. Their eyes were sunken in their sockets, and their lips were cracked and white, like they hadn't had water for days. One was busy carving the wood banister for the second floor's staircase. At first, I thought he held cherrywood, but then realized it was just covered in blood, all from his hands. He must have knocked himself a few times, but he didn't stop.

I can't stop thinking about it. I tried to break them out of whatever spell they were under but nothing worked, so I gave up and went back up to bed. Last night I heard them working, but I didn't want to go out there again. I'm still convinced it's just a dream. How can Marguerite and the children sleep through all the noise? It doesn't make sense. I must be going mad. Those workers know nothing of hard work anyway.

September 28th, 1750

The house is so close to being done.

They're beasts, truly. They must be. They don't tire, they don't drink, they don't eat. They've become the most efficient machine I've ever seen. It's unbelievable how much the house has progressed. We're getting so close.

The days are becoming colder and sometimes I'll wake up at night due to the chill in the air. The sounds of those fools working through the night used to keep me up, now it lulls me to sleep like a mother's lullaby. There is something troubling, however. I feel as if I'm being watched. Of course, there are dozens of people here every day and someone always needs my attention. But it's bigger than that and it feels… sinister. Like someone is constantly leaning over my shoulder. I don't know what to make of it.

October 4th, 1750

I wish more than anything to be away from this place. I dreamt of our flat in Paris again last night, which may be why my feelings of regret are particularly strong today. Josephine is becoming worse with every passing hour it seems, and last night was the first real night of sleep I had gotten since she fell ill. I am beyond grateful I was able to dream at last of something to calm my worn-down nerves. Marguerite is even worse than I am. She refuses to leave the poor girl.

There is a darkness over the house like a shroud, I can feel it.

October 10th, 1750

Something terrible has happened. I fear my grief has broken me. How will my family every forgive me? How will Marguerite ever look at me again?

I didn't mean to do it, of course. I didn't see him; he was in the way. I was so angry I couldn't stop myself, and even after his face popped out in front of me, it was too late.

My boy. My beautiful boy.

I couldn't help myself. They were just sitting there! They've been laying about while Josephine is weaker by the day. It's probably the goddamn chill in the house that did it. I knew they would mess something up. I was so angry. I went at one of them. Then Jonathon was there. He tried to calm me down, or something, but I turned on him. It was too late by the time I had even thought about it.

What have I done to my beautiful boy?

Marguerite won't even look at me. She hasn't told the rest of the children though, thankfully. They're already so devastated. He was their world. For God's sake, he was ours, too. That's why I've been doing this. This is what it's always been about. I did it for them, so I could keep them safe!

Last night when Marguerite threw me out of our room, I went to the carriage house and I strangled that son of a bitch. And then I strangled them all. One after another. A silent killer, like death itself moving from victim to victim. None of them stirred as I walked past. They're like animals, like they don't even care what happens to their own. It's disgusting. And to make matters worse I had to dispose of them all myself. I was up until dawn. But at last, I am free of them. They killed my boy. If they weren't so indolent, I wouldn't have gone out there! I wouldn't have gotten so mad. Jonathon would still be here.

November 4th, 1750

This house is a curse. I wish more than anything to be free of it. To be free of all of it. I feel like a prisoner here. And the days just keep getting colder. Josephine is better, but still weak, I worry she'll forever be this fragile. If the house is not completed, she won't be able to survive the winter. I can feel that fact in my bones.

Perhaps I'm the one who's cursed us.

November 15th, 1750

I can't do this anymore. What is wrong with me? I had a chance to set my family free, and I couldn't even take it.

I spent the better half of yesterday unpacking the library. Of course, right before I went up to bed, I accidentally knocked down the candelabra onto the pile of books I hadn't organized yet. Dozens of books immediately caught fire. It quickly reached the walls, and for a moment I just sat there. My heart was slamming in my chest but a part of me just wanted to watch it burn.

I was ready to die yesterday. Would that cleanse my sins? I almost did it. I almost watched my life's creation go up in flames. All I could think about was how my family would be free from this evil. How they would thank me one day for saving them from this curse.

But then I thought about Jonathon and how we would have to leave him. We couldn't exactly dig him up and bring him to Paris. No, my boy would have to stay here. The watchman at the gate of my mistakes, among nothing but rubble and ash.

At the last second, I couldn't do it. I put it out.

Does that make me a coward?

SEVENTEEN

Viviann hid in her dressing room, curled up on the chair where Evelyn usually styled her hair. She stayed up all night reading. The journal lay open in her lap.

She twisted her bracelet around her wrist again and again, trying to steady her racing heart. William, poor William. He killed his own son. And then all the workers. She thought of the undisturbed patches of moss in the center of the cemetery, surrounding William's grave. There must have been dozens of them. All *disposed* of. Viviann thought she might be sick. It was like this house was a disease, William even thought so.

She pulled out the page that had been in his original notebook, the one she found years ago. The extra page matched this new book perfectly. The year was the same; the timeline made sense.

A sound from downstairs startled the journal out of Viviann's lap, and the pages scattered all over the carpet. Julia's laugh could be heard trailing down the hallway past her dressing room, and the sharp, "Shh!" of the new nanny. The curtains were still closed but she could see the brightening sky through the sheer fabric. She rubbed her dry eyes.

Viviann crouched down and gathered the pages. While she was there, she pulled the first journal she had found from under the vanity, still wrapped up. She laid the journals side by side. The one she had recently found looked clean compared to the half-burned book next to it. She heard Julia's distinctive bubbly laughter rising from the first floor. Julia loved the library, much to Peter's delight, and Viviann could imagine the girl and the new nanny sitting on the floor just as she was.

Julia's curdling scream shot out from the library, and Viviann felt a small tremor through the house under her. Viviann jolted, but when she heard nothing else, she took a deep breath to calm herself. They needed to get ahold of that girl's screaming, Viviann thought. William's journal had put her on edge, that's all. Her focus turned to the portrait in front of her; *her* portrait, hanging above the wardrobe on the far wall. The artist had brought over the finished painting a month after Julia was born. Peter said he didn't think it really captured her beauty and thought it should be hung in one of the corridors, but she wanted it here, where she could see it every day.

She remembered Elizabeth's painting in the attic, the strangeness that wafted from the portrait, like the paint itself was alive. She shuddered, trying to shake the image out of her head.

While she reorganized William's journal entries, she cast one last look at her portrait, hoping for the nudge of courage she always felt when she saw it. This time, when she looked, her brave expression had been replaced by that of despair. Viviann drew closer to take a better look. In the painting her eyebrows were now slanted together, her mouth slightly open like she was about to scream. She looked so sad and frightened. That can't be right, Viviann thought. That's not what it looked like when the painter brought it over when he finished. That's not what it looked like even a fortnight ago. It couldn't be.

Viviann's stomach dropped nonetheless, and her rising pulse kept her feet from turning back to her chair. Julia screamed again, but this time longer. Long enough to break the spell that kept Viviann in place and bolt from her dressing room, leaving the journals. Paintings along the corridor whizzed by. Blood pumped hard in Viviann's ears. She pulled her dress to her knees to allow her to sprint to the stairs.

"Julia!" She yelled.

Maids peeked their heads out of doorways as Viviann passed. She heard the pounding footsteps of footmen as they darted from the servants' stairway to the library. When Viviann was halfway down the stairs, the library door finally came into view. Benson, Mrs. Avery, two footmen, and Peter stood frozen in the doorway.

"Julia!" Viviann screamed again. She tore her way through the servants and even elbowed Peter aside. A horrified gasp escaped her lips when she saw inside.

All eight bookshelves that used to line the library walls had fallen into the center of the room. Hundreds of books were scattered among the wreckage. It was unlike anything Viviann had seen before; like a canon had gone off and ricocheted off the walls.

Underneath the creaking of oak shelves there was a whimpering. Viviann gasped again and began tearing at the debris, trying to grasp a hold on one of the bookshelves. Peter and the footmen jumped into action.

"Quick, get the doctor!" Viviann heard Mrs. Avery yell beyond the doorway.

With the four of them, they lifted one bookshelf, and then another, to reveal a jumbled mess of books and the nanny laying face down at the bottom of the pile. Viviann knew she was dead before they even turned her over. There was a deep gash on her head and the blood covered one side of her body. Her lifeless eyes were still open, and she looked straight through them. Mrs. Avery covered her mouth but couldn't completely conceal her cry. There was another cry, softer, and coming from the center of the wreck.

"Julia!" Viviann yelled as she pointed to the source of the sound, a shifting in the shelves in the center of the room.

When Peter and the other men hoisted the shelf farther in, Viviann ducked down to push books out of the way. A small hand poked through the cloth covers. Viviann ripped at the books until

Julia's face emerged. Shouts of relief and surprise erupted and mixed with Julia's crying. Tears blurred Viviann's vision as she pulled her little girl from the pit. Viviann held the girl close to her chest, burying her face in Julia's blonde curls, which reflected the incoming light like a halo. There was a welt on the side of her forehead, but that was the only sign of injury. Her deep sobs filled the room.

Viviann watched the nanny's body be carried from the house. A sheet draped over her, but Viviann could still see her hollow eyes. She shivered from her place in the second floor's main hallway, overlooking the monstrous windows that laid in the center of the house's façade.

"Viviann," Peter said, breaking her out of her thoughts. She turned to him and the doctor.

"As I was saying," Dr. Salinger continued. "A few broken ribs are nothing when you consider the alternative. She is incredibly lucky. As for Miss..."

"Harper," "Viviann finished. "Georgina Harper."

"Yes, Miss Harper was not so lucky. Her injuries suggest she died instantly, if that's any consolation."

Viviann thought she was going to retch, right there on the carpet and the doctor's shoes, so she kept a hand over her mouth. There was a relief so deep inside her she could collapse, and the feeling of guilt that lay deeper still. She couldn't stop thinking about Georgina's eyes and imagining them as Julia's.

EIGHTEEN

The first-floor hallways were not a place Viviann spent her time. It was dark no matter the time of day, with only two candle sconces in the expanse of space. There were paintings covering every square inch of the walls. Under usual circumstances she would've felt the eyes of the portraits pushing down on her like a weight. She marched straight past them this time, no longer intimidated with their contents. It had been exactly fifteen hours since Julia's accident. *Accident.* Viviann spent the day in Julia's nursery while the girl slept, an exhausted kind of sleep that only came after so much crying. As Viviann sat there listening to her small snores, rage began to boil in her blood. It had gone too far the moment she had been knocked unconscious during the first few months in the house. Yet she had stayed. Now, Julia had almost been killed.

"But she's a Halsby," Viviann whispered, her head in her hands. The house had been content with torturing her, but never Julia. In the two and a half years since her birth not once had anything like this happened. She was a Halsby for God's sake. But then again, so was Harriet. And Marie, and Josephine. The house didn't care; they could never be heirs, and their children wouldn't bear the Halsby name.

It was this thought that forced her to the first floor. The large door to Peter's study now loomed in front of her, which she swung open without knocking.

"Viviann? What are you-" Peter stammered from behind his desk. They hadn't spoken since their fight. He shuffled the paperwork he was working on, a letter to Bradley about the new settlement the estate would be paying to the Harper's.

"We need to leave, now." Her voice was strong though her insides twisted. She stood straighter than she ever had. This was his last chance. Peter's surprise melted into a sigh. He didn't get up.

"Is this about earlier?"

"Of course, this is about earlier!" Viviann exploded. "What's wrong with you? Julia almost died. She's not safe here. We need to leave."

"Viviann, please. Benson is handling the library. They're bolting down the bookcases as we speak. Now, we can be sure nothing like that is going to happen again."

"How can you be so sure? They were already bolted down, Peter! This isn't going to help. The house wants Julia dead."

"What?" Peter outraged, snapping up from his chair. The large oil lamp on his desk shook from the force.

"It does! It's like you said, she can't inherit. The house needs a boy. And it knows as long as Julia is alive, I will not be having another baby." She sucked in a breath.

"And you're asking what's wrong with me? Viviann, you sound mad."

"This house is a disease, and you can't even see it! How do you explain what happened today?"

"Well, I…" Peter trailed off. He looked truly dumbstruck, like he hadn't thought about it until now.

"See? That's what I'm talking about. A woman is dead. Dead. And Julia could be next. *I* could be next."

"You don't know what you're talking about," Peter spat.

"How can you be so naïve? This is why Elizabeth killed herself."

"How dare you," Peter yelled, spit flying.

"This is why William killed himself! Even *he* couldn't live in this house anymore." Viviann slammed her hands down on his desk, knocking over his ink well. Black ink ballooned across the cherrywood surface.

"What?"

"William killed himself. The original Halsby. I found his journals, and all he would talk about was how much of a mistake he made coming to this house!"

A vein throbbed in Peter's forehead. "What are you talking about? What journals?"

"He said he wished he had never finished the house. He knew there was something evil here."

Peter rubbed the bridge of his nose. He looked half dead with exhaustion. "I can't keep doing this. I tried to be sensitive when you were with child, but I can't put up with these ravings anymore."

Viviann swallowed the lump in her throat. This wasn't working and they were running out of time. The realization stung. He was never going to listen to her. Not fully, not in the way she needed. She looked down at the oil lamp. Peter began walking towards the door.

William knew there was something about this house. He almost let it burn. What a mercy to them all that would've been. If William couldn't do it, then she would.

Viviann shoved the oil lamp off the desk, pushing the books it was standing on with it. It exploded when it struck the floor, setting a meter of carpet in all directions ablaze.

NINETEEN

"What are you doing?" Peter screamed, shoving past her towards the fire. Smoke billowed up from the flames. Viviann stood frozen for a moment, watching the fire spread, until she saw Peter stamp out the edges under his shoes.

"No!" Viviann shoved him aside. He crashed into the nearest bookshelf, rattling its contents.

"This house is the legacy of the Halsby family!" Peter roared. He whipped around until he saw his suit jacket draped over his chair. He used it to smother the growing fire, but it was too late. The mess that scattered the floor and lined the walls had already ignited. He couldn't smother it all. Orange flames started crawling up the fabric sleeves; he finally dropped it when his fingertips began to burn.

Viviann grabbed his hand and started to pull him to the door. "We have to go! Please, Peter, we have to leave."

He turned on her, hate glowing in his eyes the same red as the fire around them. He seized her by the shoulders and shook, like she was one of Julia's dolls. "Why would you do this? After everything I've given you!"

"Peter, we don't need this house. Let's get Julia and go while we can." She tried to wrestle free from his grasp. The smoke made the room hazy and their lungs heavy. "We can start over, just the three of us. Please, Peter."

"You're not going anywhere," he said through gritted teeth. He used one hand to clutch her by the throat, and the other to keep her in place.

Black spots bloomed in Viviann's vision, and the little bit of air she was able to swallow was full of smoke and ash. She clawed at his hand, trying to pry his thick fingers from her neck. His hold on her was too strong. His blue eyes looked black in the shadow of the fire, but his edges were fuzzy. The blood pounded in her brain, threatening to explode from her eye sockets. Tears streamed down her face and into the corners of her mouth.

With her hip pressed against the desk, Viviann's hand scuttled across its hot surface, sending all his paperwork to the floor. Her fingertips found the tip of his letter opener. Brandishing it like a knife, she slammed it into Peter's neck, sliding it all the way to the ivory handle.

Blood sputtered from the wound in thick red waves. Peter's eyes widened as his grip loosened, and Viviann fell to her knees. Black spots formed at the edges of her vision as she heard Peter choke on his own blood. He stumbled through the smoky room until he collapsed, just a few feet from Viviann. His desperate stare burned into her as blood coated his right side, drenching both hands that were clutching his wound. His mouth opened but only drops of blood escaped his lips.

The pounding in Viviann's ears drowned any noise from the room. Her lungs ached against the smoke she sucked in. Tears gushed down her soot covered cheeks, and a sob escaped her throat as she watched her husband take his last few breaths. It looked like he was trying to say something, but his severed vocal cords wouldn't allow it.

"I'm sorry," she cried, unable to raise her voice above a whisper.

Peter reached out with his bloody hand, palm up like he was asking for something. All the color began draining from his face. Viviann reached back and grasped the few fingers she could reach. His grip was weak, and the blood was hot between their hands.

"I'm so sorry," she said again, "I'm sorry I couldn't love you."

The flames crept over Peter's legs. She had to force herself to pull away from him. Sweat dripped down her brow in the oven-like room. A tear rolled down Peter's temple. Viviann was running out the door as the fire consumed the rest of his body.

Viviann could breathe much easier as she exploded through the hallway, pulling her skirts to her knees. The hem was dotted with scorch marks and her sleeve was covered in Peter's blood. She couldn't think about any of it; all that mattered now was Julia.

She made it to the grand staircase and took the steps two at a time. As her feet sprang from each step, she felt the wood beneath her begin to sag and buckle. She gripped the banister for support with a gasp, almost losing her footing. Casting a look behind her, she found the steps rotting along her path. Dark mold spores sprouted on the carpet with ferocity, but she was quicker, clearing the landing before the stairs gave out underneath her. The house knew what she'd done.

"Fire!" She heard someone call and remembered there was a house full of servants beneath her. Her breath caught and she stopped dead in her tracks. She heard Benson's booming voice shout demands, and her guilt eased. He would make sure everyone got out. She continued in her sprint towards the nursery.

She made it to the threshold to find Julia's crib empty. Viviann whipped her head around the room. "Julia!" She screamed. She thought she might faint as she thrashed through the empty blankets in the crib. Where else could she be?

On a whim Viviann dashed towards her bedroom. Through the open door she saw Evelyn holding Julia to her chest, calling for Viviann.

"Evelyn!" Viviann yelled in relief. She ran faster; she wanted nothing more than to feel Julia against her, to smell her and hear her voice. The doors that were open around her began slamming shut. First the morning room across the hall, then the first guest room, then the nursery.

"Evelyn, the door!"

Evelyn whipped around as the door started to close. Viviann

shoved her way through the threshold as it slammed, pinning her to the door jam. She cried out as the door pushed against her, threatening to cut her in half. Evelyn set Julia down as she ran to her mistress. Her eyes were so wide they could have burst.

Without speaking, Evelyn slammed her body weight into the door, moving it an inch. Viviann pushed with all the might of her one hand that had cleared the doorway, while her other hand scratched at the wall it was trapped against. Their eyes locked. The pressure on her chest eased by another inch, and Viviann scraped through the small opening. As she made it past, the door gave one final shove and slammed closed, knocking Evelyn to the ground.

"Come on! We have to go!" Viviann scooped Evelyn up and ran towards Julia, before her skirt pulled her back, half of her dress caught between the door. Viviann giggled the door handle in vain. Locked. She tried tearing the skirt at the seams, but it was sturdy and wouldn't yield to her clawing fingers.

Evelyn jumped into action without a word, tearing at the buttons down the back. The bodice slipped off her chest. Viviann ripped her arms out of the sleeves, glad to be free of the thick fabric and the bloody reminder of her deed. Evelyn untied the crinoline skirt and Viviann was free. She stumbled across the room in her underpetticoat and corset. She was glad the door was closed.

Viviann wrapped her arms around Julia and felt the little girl's hair tickle her cheek.

"What's going on?" Evelyn blurted. "Where were you?"

Viviann picked Julia up and carried her towards the large

window overlooking the front of the house. Small wisps of black smoke wafted from beneath the bedroom door. "I set the fire. We need to get out of here."

"What? W-why would you do that? Where's Lord Halsby?"

Viviann felt a stab in her heart at the reminder. She turned to reveal her tear-streaked face. She gave a small shake of her head, a twitch, and Evelyn knew. She could see the bruises already forming on Viviann's neck. The maid brought her hands to her face as if in prayer. Her dark eyes welled with her own tears. Viviann turned back to the window, still holding Julia, and tried the window's lock, but the clasp wouldn't budge. Smart house.

"Why, my lady?" Evelyn whispered.

"Didn't you see what happened yesterday? The house was going to kill her." Viviann tightened her hold on her daughter.

"So you set a fire? Now we're trapped, my lady. There must've been a better way- "

"There was no other way!" Viviann yelled, slamming her fist against the window's glass. It didn't crack, but the noise made Julia burst into loud sobs and Evelyn jump. A soft haze shadowed the room, and the smell of burning grew stronger every second.

"This house is a disease," Viviann said.

Evelyn's shoulders slumped, and she knew she was right. The maid clutched the bridge of her nose, sucking in her fear. She met Viviann's eye. "How do we get out of here?"

"Help me with the sofa. It's okay, sweetheart, I'm just going to let you down for a second," Viviann cooed as Julia's screams raised an octave. "It's okay, I promise. Just let Mummy handle this."

Viviann hurried to the seating area across the room. It was a mad idea, but it was the only one she had. She could hear things breaking downstairs. She could hear the crumbling bits of furniture turning to dust, the paintings, worth thousands of pounds through the years, blackened and then burned in the inferno coming for them.

Viviann reached under one of the large sitting chairs, waiting for Evelyn to take the other side. "As hard as you can," she huffed, as Evelyn tried lifting the opposite end. They rushed to the window and tossed the piece of furniture as best they could. Glass exploded around them. They heard the ornate chair crash to the ground floor a second later, and a few screams from some servants below.

Viviann peered through the opening, spotting several servants in the sea of black that was the front lawn, looking up at the house with horror-stricken faces. It was a long way down. The orange glow of flames illuminated a portion of the path directly below the window. Flowerless rose bushes separated the path from the house.

"Mummy!" Julia screamed. Her pudgy finger pointed towards the door. Plumes of thick black smoke rushed through the crack beneath the door. How had it gotten to them so quickly?

"The sheets!" Viviann called, running back to the bed and throwing the pillows to the side. Julia rushed to her side and clung to her robe. "It's alright, baby. It's going to be alright."

The house creaked all around them, like a scream itself. Evelyn and Viviann didn't pause, instead they tore the sheets clean off the mattress and started tying them together. The floor beneath them shuddered under their weight. The room below them must be completely engulfed by now.

"Go stand by the window, Julia," Viviann instructed as she pulled the sheets as taut as she could, forcing her attention on the task in front of her. She hurried Evelyn to the window as well. She started tying one end of their makeshift rope around the maid's waist.

"What are you doing?" Evelyn panicked.

"You're going to take Julia and I'm going to slowly let you guys down."

"No! My lady, I can't- "

"We'll be too heavy for you to lift. Just do it." Even Julia stopped crying at the ferocity in Viviann's voice. She was mistress of the house again, and Evelyn, her maid. She finished her knot. "Please, just do it."

Evelyn situated herself on the window frame, one of her legs clearing the house. A lantern that sat on Viviann's bedside table shattered as it hit the ground. The table toppled over next, one of its legs falling through the crumbling floor.

With her eyes full of tears, Viviann gave Julia to Evelyn, kissing the girl's cheek hard one last time.

"Hold on to me tight, and don't let go. No matter what," Evelyn made Julia promise.

"Mummy!" The little girl screamed when she saw Viviann was staying behind.

"It's okay, sweetheart, do what Evelyn says. I'll be right behind you." Viviann tied the other end of the blanket around her own waist, in case her hands ever gave out. The smoke climbed down her throat and into her lungs.

Evelyn had both feet out of the window and started to climb out. Viviann twisted the blanket around herself a few times to tighten the hold. Evelyn gingerly put her full body weight out of the window. Viviann cried out at the force, but it held.

"Go, go!" Viviann yelled, her hands burning and her arms already shaking.

Evelyn held on to the blankets tight and used her feet to scale down the house's front. She heard the screams of the other servants behind her, and the hot breath of Julia at her neck.

"It's okay, I've got you. Your mummy's coming," Evelyn repeated, mostly to calm herself. She watched Viviann's face shrink as she lifted them down. The extent of the fire was apparent just a few meters into their descent. Fire raged against the windows, almost all of them broken, and it was impossible to see anything beyond the flames. The stones around the openings grew black with ash.

Evelyn crossed through the ivy that scaled the house, the bits that hadn't burned away, and felt her foot catch in one of its branches. She tried tugging it away, but the plant held strong. A single vine wrapped itself around her ankle and travelled up her leg with amazing speed. The vine found its way to Julia and tried twisting around the little girl's leg.

"No!" Evelyn screamed, ripping her foot from the ivy's grasp and kicking at the rogue vine. She looked behind her. Would they survive if she let them drop?

The vine had a hold on Julia, and the girl started to slip out of Evelyn's grasp. Viviann watched from above. Red flames crawled up the walls behind her, and she felt the hotness on her back like she would alight next. They were running out of time.

One of the footmen, Henry, climbed the ivy from the ground level, trying to reach Julia and Evelyn. She could see Evelyn pulling at the vines with all her might. Where one would snap, another would start climbing. The crackling of fire roared in Viviann's ears, and she knew in seconds the room would be completely ablaze.

Viviann ripped at the tied blankets around her and let go. The blanket exploded out of her hands and out of sight. Evelyn and Julia plummeted towards the ground with a scream. The force snapped the vines holding them and they crashed into the roses bellow, swallowed by leaves and thorns. Henry helped pull them from the planter with disregard to injuries, and soon they were lying on the gravel. Bloody, but alive.

The burning walls surrounding the window frame forced Viviann to take her exit. The bottom of her underpetticoat was burnt, as well as little bits of her shoes. She didn't have a plan. There was no blanket to carry her down, and the ivy was too far away to scale either. She was going to have to jump. Her palms burned where they still gripped the frame. It was now or never.

She lifted herself down and braced her feet against the worn sides of the house. She was weaker than she thought; one of her hands slipped from the edge. She held on with her other hand as long as she could, the tips of her shoes scrapping the stone surrounding her. She felt something around her ankle. Vines swarmed Viviann's leg while she hovered between life and death.

She let go of the ledge. Smoky air whirled past her as she fell and she finally saw the full extent of the fire. The vines that swarmed her slowed her descent, snapping and growing as rapidly as her free fall, but they weren't strong enough to hold her.

Viviann struck the rose bed feet first, and pain shot through one of her legs when she met solid ground. Sounds were cut from her ears as the pain swelled and flashes of light bounced around her eyelids. Two pairs of hands pulled from her underarms, pain surging through her clouded head.

Benson and Charlie dragged her as far away from the house as they could, the thorns tearing her slip further. Mrs. Avery cradled Julia, trying to soothe her wails, and Henry had an unconscious Evelyn in his arms.

Behind them, the once great Halsby manor was engulfed in bright red and orange flames. The fire pounded through the facade, swallowing everything inside, while screams echoed in the hollow space.

They felt a rumbling beneath their feet and knew it to be the house. It was too late. The remaining ivy dripping from the house's second story windows looked like tears running down a stone face.

ACKNOWLEDGMENTS

This book would not have been possible without my mentors, Dr. Kim Vose and Dr. Mary Adler, two of the smartest women I know. So much gratitude to Dr. Bob Mayberry, whose feedback and patience brought back my passion, and to Dr. Kendall McClellan, who introduced me to gothic literature in the first place. I am indebted to the great gothic writers, Edgar Allan Poe and Daphne Du Maurier, for supplying me with the steppingstones to write this novel.

Channel Islands' English Club, specifically Brian Whalen, Sarah Feldhut, Yoselin Edith Aguilar, Philip Carrigan, Federico Guzman, and Marina Simms kept me sane from the beginning with their endless encouragement and thoughtful comments.

The biggest thank you to Jayden Harper, who helped with so many technical issues along the way, and the immensely talented Alexander Stott, who designed the perfect cover for this novel.

I'd like to thank Jennifer Johnsen, Samantha Thompson, Kelly Cronander, and Meredith Quinn for their support, ideas, inspiration, and motivation. Lastly, thank you to my mother, father, stepmother, and nonna for never doubting me.

www.ingramcontent.com/pod-product-compliance
Ingram Content Group UK Ltd.
Pitfield, Milton Keynes, MK11 3LW, UK
UKHW022021190726
13853UKWH00005B/2038

9 798463 775344